BUILI

UNIVER

Aldona Grupas

Nurse Stories

ISBN 9791220141888
First edition: September 2023

Nurse Stories

Introduction

Dear reader, my name is Aldona Grupas. I am a nurse with almost forty years of experience in healthcare and I have been working in England since 2005, caring for the sick and elderly. As you might expect, I have a lot of experience in this field, and would like to share some of it with you.

There are three main fields of interest in my life:

1. Healthcare – specifically for the elderly.

2. Literature—I enjoy writing and sharing my experience as well as those of my patients and colleagues, and have already published two books. One is about the Lithuanian community in the West Midlands: *The Lithuanian Community in the West Midlands after the Second World War*, and the other is about my work experience as a nurse in England and is entitled, *Nurse, Give Me a Pill for Death*.

The book which you are reading now is a collection of true stories from my life, which also contains pieces of advice for those who act as caregivers for bedridden people. Whilst you won't find anything revelatory in this book, you will find useful and practical information to use in such situations. The purpose of this book is to relate to the stories of real people, so that by reading them you may find a new approach and a way out of difficult situations. Perhaps these stories will give you answers to your questions, and thus you will be able to stay calm, healthy and confident whilst taking care of your loved one.

I would like to start with a story which has determined the course of my life.

Tights for Sale

Klaipeda

At the end of the 1980s, a business sprang up in Lithuania producing what became known as "consumer goods". I decided to join the ranks of these new entrepreneurs, and became involved in a business that was becoming trendy: sewing women's tights. I bought myself a sewing machine and put it in the kitchen. With my new workspace set up, I was ready to make my first million.

It turned out that someone I knew, a girl who worked at the local clinic called Bronya, was also making all sorts of beautiful creations on her own sewing machine. We became friends, and she taught me how to make tights from yarns of wool. After two or three lessons, I began to sew these in-demand garments myself. I enjoyed thinking up different patterns and sewing them into the design. The end result was some beautiful white tights with lace patterns on the sides. But every woman in Klaipeda already had tights like those. Where could I find more legs to put my creations on?

My mother wrote to a friend of hers, Olya, who lived in Alma-Ata (present-day Almaty) in Kazakhstan. Letters travelled quickly in those days, and we soon received a reply from her, with an invitation for me to visit her. Olya told us that the only people selling tights in Alma-Ata were a couple of Latvian ladies in the bazaar. Here was my chance to start an international business! I bought 200 new pairs of tights from other seamstresses, then went straight to the Aeroflot office and bought a ticket to Alma-Ata, with a return flight two weeks later.

The day when I would become an international business-woman arrived. It began with a journey from Klaipeda to Vilnius airport, then a flight from Vilnius to Alma-Ata, with four stops: in Moscow, Tula, and two other towns. I don't remember which ones, but I do remember that it was February, and freezing cold. At the airport in Tula we had to step off the plane and into a waiting room. It was -40°C outside, and I was only wearing a thin jacket. I had never been so cold in my life!

Alma-Ata
At that time Almaty was still called Alma-Ata, and was still the capital of Kazakhstan. I arrived in the middle of the night, and there was no-one to meet me. A taxi took me to the address I would be staying at – a communal building in a neighbourhood far from the centre of the town, with hostel beds. There were no streetlights, and it was pitch black; I didn't know which door to knock on. Thankfully, the taxi driver helped me find my entrance, using his cigarette lighter to guide us through the dark-ness. I knocked on a door and was let inside.

I had never met Olya before, but I recognised her from her photo. She was tall, very slim, and blonde, with short hair and blue eyes. She realised who I was straight away, and apologised for not having come to the airport to meet me. For some reason, she thought I wasn't coming. I thought this was odd, because I had even sent her a tele-gram with my flight number and the time I would land. But never mind: the important thing was that I was there. A tiny apartment (two rooms and a kitchen with a heated stove) in a giant communal living space; I was thankful to have a corner of the spare room for myself.

Early in the morning, Olya's parents were already making a fuss turning on the stove, both to make breakfast, and so that their guest would be warm enough. They were a wonderful elderly couple: the father was a veteran of the Second World War, and the mother was a pensioner. Olya taught Russian language and literature at the Kazakh state university.

Olya's mother made some traditional Kazakh dishes: *manty*, *beshbarmak* and *sorpa*. I especially liked the manty, which looked just like the vareniki I was used to it, but tasted completely different. To make them they added pumpkin, onion, garlic and spices to lamb mince, and boiled them together in a special pan. Delish! And to think that at home in Lithuania I couldn't stand the taste of lamb. Olya's parents gave me tea with milk, wild apricot jam, and something similar to blini pancakes, called *shelpeki*. I thought pancakes were the same all over the world, but no – Olya's mother made these ones in a tall-rimmed, thick cooking pot called a *kazan*. I had never seen a pan like this before, and I still remember how those *shelpeki* tasted on those early February mornings in Alma-Ata.

I was also surprised by how people in Alma-Ata bought milk. To get your hands on just one litre, you needed to get up at 5 in the morning and stand in a queue. Olya's father explained that they bought powdered milk from a shop, mixed it with boiling water, and then added some natural milk to it. Were there no cows in Kazakhstan? I also tried the national drink, *kumys* (mare's milk), but I didn't like it – it tasted sour, like milk that has gone off. I learned that Kazakhs even eat horses. This country never ceased to amaze me…

Olya introduced me to one of their neighbours, a young girl called Izat, who agreed to show me the town, and take me to the famous Green Bazaar.

We went on a tram. Nearer to the centre, there were tall apartment blocks, their facades decorated with concrete slabs of various colours. Apparently, these were so that the sun wouldn't shine into the rooms during the very hot summers. They also helped to keep the buildings intact during earthquakes. Goodness me, were there earthquakes too?

When we arrived at the Green Bazaar, aromas from the east were drifting through it. The main scent was the smell of apples. We had a lot of apples in Lithuania too, but I had never tried the kind that was found in Alma-Ata: a sort called the *Aport*. Alma-Ata means "father of apples" in Kazakh. My head was spinning from the mountains of spices, herbs, apricots and raisins! It was the first time I had ever seen carrots prepared Korean-style: rubbed with oil and herbs, then sliced into little strips. I thought they had been brought from Korea; Izat laughed at this, but she didn't tell me why they are called 'Korean'...

The spices and vegetables were all sold in the covered pavilion in the centre of the bazaar – but to sell our tights we had to stand outside in the freezing cold. I had imagined lines of women queuing up to buy them, and selling all 200 pairs in a flash. It didn't quite happen like that: by lunchtime we had sold all of four pairs. What could I do? A woman seller standing next to us said that I should try to sell my tights to a department store instead.

14

Almaty's central department store was a huge place. I wandered through it, taking a look at everything, until I found the right department. Everyone spoke in Russian, and everything was written in Russian too. Didn't Kazakhs have their own language?

The manager of the store was a Russian woman, getting on in years, with a stack of chestnut hair on top of her head. I told her my business proposal, showed her the tights, and she very kindly agreed to buy them for her department. She called another manager, Zamira, into her office, introduced us, and told her to take my tights.

I went back to Izat at the bazaar and gave her my news. She was still freezing outside, but was in a good mood: she had sold 10 more pairs.

I told her how surprised I was that all Kazakhs spoke Russian. She explained to me that Kazakhstan began to be "russified" when the country's Kazakh population shrank in the 1930s. Many people were deported to Kazakhstan by Stalin, and almost all of them spoke Russian. These new arrivals worked on the land; this is how the Russian language arrived in Kazakhstan.

The next day I brought another 50 pairs of tights to the department store, to see if I could sell them as well. With our sales going well, Izat and I could afford a little free time, and we decided to see some more of Alma-Ata. As we walked around, the town surprised me again: all the fountains were working. Their water was still flowing, even as the mountains that surround Alma-Ata were covered in ice. In Lithuania they would turn the fountains off in the winter. Had Alma-Ata never had a frozen winter before, and this was the first time it had ever been this cold?

Before leaving Lithuania, I had dreamed about drinking real eastern coffee in a real eastern country. But I was mistaken – everywhere I went people were drinking tea. On my third day I was missing coffee so much that the minute I spotted a cafeteria, I dashed inside. Behind the bar stood a tall, handsome, fair-haired young man, who looked like he was pouring coffee into a glass. Goodness me, coffee in a glass? Was this a Kazakh tradition? When I got to the front of the queue I asked for a glass of coffee. But the young man acted as if he hadn't heard me, and he kept ignoring me even when I repeated myself. I got angry, and asked him impatiently:

- Why aren't you serving me? Do I look that bad?

He smiled and replied:

- Miss, you look wonderful. But I'm not going to give you any coffee…

My jaw must have hit the floor.

- Why not?
- Because this drink is made from chicory.
-

I never did drink coffee in Alma-Ata...

The next morning it was back to work at the bazaar. We stood in the cold, sold some of our tights, then went for a delicious lunch. Olya's mother had instructed us not to be late home, and to save some room for dinner, but I couldn't walk past all these eastern treats, which were prepared on the street in front of my eyes.

We worked at the market for another four days. On the last day an Uzbek man approached me (I had already learned to tell Uzbeks from Kazakhs) and asked to buy 10 pairs of tights. Yes! But I didn't have that many left. He got angry, and muttered something; all I could make out was that he had seven daughters.

A week had passed, and all my tights were gone. I had earned a little from my sales at the bazaar, and would receive my money from the department store when they had sold all the pairs that they had taken from me.

I didn't need to go back to the Green Bazaar. I could walk some more around the town, go up to the Medeo ice rink, take a look inside the Indian shop, and have a meal in a restaurant. Fabulous!

Izat bought us tickets to the theatre that evening, and in the morning, she took me to the Indian shop. I was having withdrawal symptoms without coffee, but even in 'Ganga' (Ganges) there was no coffee. I bought myself a few trinkets, and some presents for my friends: bracelets, bead necklaces, rings and earrings.

In the evening we went to the theatre. There was a giant chandelier hanging in the middle of the hall, and a large, beautiful staircase leading to the balcony, where we had seats in the first row. The play was harrowing: a tragedy about the Stalinist era, in which the KGB arrested a scientist, and tortured him into confessing to a crime he didn't commit. I finally managed to hear the Kazakh language spoken, and there was a synchronised translation into Russian through headphones. I was surprised again at how liberal the Kazakhs were; at that time it would have been impossible to put on a play like this in Lithuania.

I eventually got my hands on a long-awaited cup of coffee, at the Medeo ice rink. It was a cold but sunny day. An old minibus (we didn't have ones like this in Lithuania anymore) was spluttering so much that I thought we would have to get out and push it up the hill. But to my surprise it made it, to this famous high-altitude complex, a factory for skating records. In the distance were snow-capped mountains; the bright sun was high in the sky, and next to us was a mountain named Mokhnatka, its mighty pine trees standing to attention, like dark green soldiers defending their territory. It was all indescribably beautiful.

After admiring the view our next stop was the Medeo restaurant. And finally, some coffee – a cup of Indian instant. I thought it was a bit weak, so I asked for my second cup to be a little stronger. And after this second cup, of course I couldn't deny myself a third. The caffeine hit felt like heaven!

After Medeo we went back to the town, and Izat took me to a traditional Kazakh restaurant. The place reminded me of a train carriage: on the right-hand side were high windows, and on the left, just like in the second-class 'kupe' carriages, were cabins with a low table and cushions to sit on, sewed with beautiful multicoloured patterns. We went to an empty cabin, took off our boots and fur coats, and sat down on the cushions. We were brought some bowls of beshbarmak... but there was no cutlery on the table.

- How can we eat it without a knife and fork? - I asked.

Smiling, Izat explained:

- The word beshbarmak means "five fingers". You eat it with your hands!

But I wasn't used to eating like this, so I asked the waiter to bring me some cutlery. Meanwhile, Izat told me how Kazakhs make authentic beshbarmak. I was enjoying my meal until I heard the words 'sheep's head', 'horse meat', and even 'camel meat'...

- I am not going to eat anything's head! – I said, indignantly.
- Don't worry, restaurants don't make beshbarmak with animals' heads.

But I had already lost my appetite.

The next day I went back to the department store, and was overjoyed when they told me that all my tights had been sold. We decided to celebrate the end of my business trip, and reserved a table at a restaurant.

The restaurant was full. In the middle of the dining hall was a table adorned with fruits and sweets. Fruits in February!

Our waiter, a young Kazakh, asked:

- Where are you from?
- I'm from Lithuania.
- Ah, I know Riga: I served in the army there.
- No, no, Riga is Latvia! I'm from Lithuania: Vilnius...

We laughed, and I ordered some sparkling wine and a fancy-sounding platter. The waiter brought my sparkling wine with a little plate of some sliced meats.

- And where is the platter? – I exclaimed.
- Right there! – the waiter replied, pointing at the little plate.
-

Oh goodness! A platter in Kazakhstan wasn't quite so grand as it is elsewhere. It taught me a lesson: when you choose a dish, read the menu carefully to see what it is made of.

But it didn't matter! We drank sparkling wine, ate our little selection of meats, I was invited to dance, and I was happy at how everything had turned out. As Shakespeare wrote in Hamlet: "There are more things in heaven and earth, Horatio, than are dreamt of in your philosophy."

The next day I collected my money from the account's office at the department store. There was a little less than I expected, but I took it as their commission for making my life so much easier. Everything has to be paid for. I said goodbye to my new friends, Izat took me to the airport, and I flew back home.

What happens now?

At home again in Lithuania after my trip to Alma-Ata, all the discussions in our republic were about independence. All across the Soviet Union factories were beginning to shut down; there was a shortage of wool to make tights with. In fact, there was a shortage of everything. My new business ceased to be, before I had a chance to make my million.

And so, we began to fight for our independence from the Soviet empire, which by now was in complete disarray. In Lithuania a civic movement called Sąjūdis was born, which lobbied for the country to regain its independence. All Lithuanians read the Sąjūdis newspaper; we couldn't stop asking each other: "What happens now?"

In January 1990 the Soviet army was sent into Lithuania. On 12 January Sąjūdis called the nation to a mass protest in Vilnius. Crowds of people gathered outside important buildings: the Seimas (parliament), the radio tower, the television centre. There was another protest in Klaipeda. Soviet tanks burst into the city's main square, and the streets were filled with armed soldiers. Walking past them was unpleasant, not to mention frightening. Citizens of Klaipeda began to gather in the evenings by the city's Communist Party headquarters. They stayed even when it got dark, and set up a television screen to watch what was happening in Vilnius. And goodness, what was happening in Vilnius! People began to fight with the army, but at about 11 o'clock one night the soldiers took control of the television stations and cut off all the broadcasts. After that we had no way of getting news from the capital. Would there really be a war for independence? In Klaipeda the tanks and soldiers didn't move from the square. Of course, I was one of those standing outside the Communist Party building, and was waiting for any kind of news that would calm my nerves. I lived nearby, so I would boil water at home and bring tea for everyone. At about 1 or 2 in the morning someone from the Seimas came onto the radio and announced that the soldiers hadn't taken over the parliament; instead, negotiations were being held with the Communist leaders. On the morning of the 13th of January, the television showed the harrowing events of the previous night; we learned that some people had even lost their lives. On the 8th of February Lithuania refused to recognise the Soviet constitution anymore, and the decision of the Seimas from 1940 to become part of the Soviet Union.

In the spring of 1990 no-one understood what was happening. Businesses started to close, including the mud baths where I worked as a massage therapist. I had to make ends meet somehow, and this is where my experience of selling tights saved me. My friend Bronya suggested making some money selling flowers, before Women's Day on 8 March. Her idea was to travel to Murmansk with some tulips. Of course, I said yes!

Murmansk
It wasn't hard to find people who were growing tulips: for the Women's Day holiday each year all men buy flowers for the women in their lives. Bronya and I just needed to choose some good ones, and keep them fresh until 8 March. We packed the tulips into eight big boxes and kept them on my balcony, in the hope that they would not bloom too early. But in order to transport them into Russia, we needed to obtain a permit from the epidemiology lab. Bronya delegated this job to me:

- You're a medic; you'll be better at speaking to other medics…

But I was used to treating people, not flowers. Anyway, I went to see the epidemiologists. I paid them their fee, and they gave me the permit without so much as looking at the tulips.

We managed to buy tickets for a flight to Murmansk from Kaliningrad. Bronya's friend Zhenya drove us to Kaliningrad in his minibus, with our boxes of flowers crammed into the back seats. The staff at the airport were appalled at how much luggage we were carrying with us, and shouted at us that we couldn't take that many boxes. I went up to the two men who were loading the suitcases onto the plane and said:

- Guys, you'll take all of these boxes for me, won't you? We're taking tulips to Murmansk for Women's Day…
- So women are doing business now? Why don't you leave that to the men and stay at home? – the older man asked.
- I lost my job and need to make a living – that's why I'm not at home…
- Whatever you say. Give me 50 roubles and we'll take your boxes.

Oh goodness, 50 roubles! It was a lot, but I paid him, and they loaded our flowers onto the plane.

In Murmansk we were met by a man called Igor, who was married to Bronya's friend Marina. Four of our boxed fitted into his car, and the other four went in a taxi. The snow was waist-high, and the trees that grew by the side of the road looked like toy models. It turns out that trees don't grow very tall in Murmansk because it is so cold for most of the year. It was still very cold outside, and slippery; several times I had to slide down a hill on my bottom. On one of the hills stands the 'Alyosha' monument, a memorial to those who defended the Arctic during the Second World War.

Marina and Igor lived on the seventh floor of a monolithic flat block. I was surprised that their home was so warm, when I couldn't see any radiators. They told me that the heating pipes are built into the walls. Because the flat was so warm, it was also very dry, and every night they would hang wet bed sheets in every room to make sure there was moisture in the air. It was good that they had an enclosed balcony, otherwise our tulips would have either frozen, or bloomed too early in the warm rooms.

At the local market, some sellers – from Latvia; where else? – were already selling tulips. We wanted to set up shop next to them, but it turned out that everything was controlled by the Azerbaijanis: you needed to ask for permission to sell things – and of course you needed to pay. We found their boss, an extremely slimy and rude man, who offered to buy all of our flowers for the same price as we had bought them in Lithuania.

- You can get stuffed! - said Bronya, with a hand gesture thrown in for good measure. The Azerbaijani shrugged his shoulders and walked away.

We were losing heart. It was 7 March, the day before Women's Day, and if we didn't sell our tulips today then we might as well throw them away. We decided to go and stand next to a supermarket. We took one box of flowers, wrapped the bouquets in some paper, and carefully carried them out of the market.

People started to buy them, and everything was going well. But then Bronya, her teeth chattering from the cold, had a brilliant idea:

-   Go and make a deal with the manager of the supermarket…

I went inside and found the woman in charge. As soon as she learned that I was from Lithuania, her face lit up and she gave me a hug, as if I was a long-lost relative. It turned out that her son-in-law was from Kaunas. In distant Murmansk, me being from Klaipeda practically made me family too. The lady, Valentina, gave us some space in the supermarket, a table, and a bucket of water for the tulips. She wouldn't accept a kopeck from us in return.

At 9 the next morning we were standing in the most visible part of the shop, and were ready to bloom ourselves, so happy were we. Things had worked out again! There were no scary Azerbaijanis here, and our tulips sold like hot cakes – by 11 all our boxes were empty. The only angry customers were the ones that were unhappy we hadn't brought more flowers. But we didn't mind: our handbags were now filled with roubles, and we were delighted with our new business. We gave one bouquet of tulips to the lovely Valentina, and in return she handed us several jars of crab meat and some crab sticks. We had never eaten crab in Lithuania; we had only heard about how good it tasted.

That evening, Marina's father made us a special porridge made from three types of seeds: millet, buckwheat and barley. When Marina and Igor got home from work we all sat down to dinner together. I had never tried porridge like this before, but I enjoyed it. There was plenty to drink as well. But Bronya and I were missing home, and asked Igor to take us back to the airport.

The airport was almost empty, but as often happened, we were told there were no tickets to anywhere in the Baltics. I slid 50 roubles inside my passport and walked up to the desk again. The now-smiling girl behind the counter suddenly found two tickets to Minsk...

It was a late flight, leaving at 11 at night. The plane was half-empty. I had a row of three seats to myself, so I lay down and slept. After a journey from Minsk airport to its train station, a train to Vilnius and a bus to Klaipeda, I got home in the evening of the 9th of March.

In the morning of the 11th of March 1990, the supreme council of the Lithuanian Soviet Socialist Republic announced that the republic had ceased to be part of the Soviet Union. It was the first Soviet republic to gain its independence. As it turned out, I had left Soviet Lithuania with some tulips, and had come back with some money, to the independent country of Lithuania.

A country with many faces

Integration with Europe

Three years passed. In Lithuania life changed at a heady pace. Our old socialist values were ripped up, while new, capitalist ideas were only beginning to take root. The idea of independence became tied to pronouncements about adopting western values, getting rid of the rouble, and introducing our own currency - the *litas*. Independent Lithuania found herself at a very beneficial crossroads of trade routes. Our integration with Europe went full speed ahead.

My personal 'Euro-integration' was also gathering speed. In these years I went back to Germany and Poland a few more times. , and made several friends in each place. Europe became closer and easier to understand. Meanwhile, in my own country, the era of the first accumulation of capital had begun, with everything that came with it: the transfer of state property into private hands, crime out of control, violence between gangs, unemployment, cruel pyramid schemes…

Cars became a popular business. The more savvy of us travelled to Germany, Poland or Holland, bought second-hand cars and brought them back to Lithuania to sell. Some even went to the United States, and sent cars back to Klaipeda in shipping containers.

Amsterdam

In 1995 I decided to go to Holland - or the Netherlands, as it's now correct to call it. I knew a man called Vitas who owned a minibus, and he used to regularly take groups of young men to Utrecht to haul used cars to

Lithuania. One time he took me along with them. For the men it was an ordinary trip to buy cars at the auto market; I was the only woman among them, and the only tourist.

The eight or nine of us squeezed into the minibus, and Vitas took us on the roads through Europe: Lithuania - Russia - Poland - Germany - the Netherlands. It was a well-trodden path: the Iron Curtain had long since fallen, and the border guards knew exactly why the groups of Lithuanian men were going to Holland, so there were never any problems at borders.

Along the way I looked out, half-interested, at the German and Polish landscapes. The roads of North Rhine-Westphalia and Lower Saxony no longer left me in awe, as they once had. It was the same autobahns, the same neat houses with tiled roofs, and the same windmills, forests and fields.

And so, we arrived in *Nederland*, which for me was like something out of a fairytale. My first impressions were of a huge number of rivers, canals and old bridges. I had always imagined Holland as a country of tulips and canals - but as I got to know it, I understood that it is a country with many faces; one that can't be defined in such simple terms.

On the way I convinced the men to go via Amsterdam. I was desperate to spend some time in the capital, to see this famous city of sin, and the just as well-known Keukenhof botanical garden. It wouldn't be a long detour: Vitas said that there was only about 40km between Utrecht and Amsterdam. The young men, of course, didn't mind taking a look at the girls in Amsterdam's red-light district one more time. In the end, no detour was needed: the highway our minibus was travelling on, the Snelweg A1, took us straight to Amsterdam.

The famous De-Valletes district is in the very centre of the city, close to the port. Since the 14th century sailors have used it for docking services, but now these narrow, old, cobblestone-covered streets are a magnet for tourists. The best part begins at dusk: illuminations, music, a crowd of tourists, and on all sides - behind apartment windows lit up in red - sit prostitutes of all shapes, sizes and skin tones, perched on tall bar stools. *O mijn God!* Being from the port of Klaipeda I had heard plenty about prostitutes who provide their services to sailors. I even recognised some of them in the street. But for it to be so open, so on display for the public to see, I had never seen before. And here the men I had travelled with were staring, salivating, and giving cat calls.

It also amazed me that in Holland it was legal to sell cannabis. The Dutch call it 'weed' or 'hash', and some imaginative Russian tourists have thought to call it not 'marijuana', but *Maria Ivanovna*. And if you wanted to try it – no problem! You can buy weed (or sweets, cookies or chewing gum with weed inside) everywhere: in supermarkets, in bars, in pharmacies, and you can smoke a ready-made joint with a cup of coffee in any of a number of coffee shops. This is what I did. I bought a joint for 10 Dutch guilders and a coffee for nine. The young waiter rolled it for me himself, and brought it to me on a silver tray. Maybe it wasn't very good *Maria Ivanovna*, or maybe my brain wasn't receptive enough to it, but I enjoyed the coffee more, and the quiet music in the background…

The next morning, when my male companions gathered around the minibus, I didn't know if their eyes were red from a sleepless night, or from weed. But in Amsterdam, Holland really seemed like a country of marijuana!

I wandered around the car market, only looking at the cars, because I didn't know how to buy one. I paid more attention to what was happening around them. I was interested to see how people lived - those who were selling and those who were buying. My companions already knew a lot, and showed me more of Holland.

I came to a firm conclusion: the Dutch love freedom, in everything!

Keukenhof
On the way to Utrecht, we stopped in the little town of Lisse, near Amsterdam, to visit the famous botanical gardens of Keukenhof. I had been dreaming of seeing the world's biggest tulip garden with my own eyes. And here I was, in this fairytale country, immersed in a sea of tulips of all different colours and sorts. What beauty! The flowers left me in an indescribable wonder: red, yellow, light blue, violet, and even black tulips! The flower shows looked as if they came from the canvas of the most brilliant artist, but they were really the surprising work of Dutch plant breeders, who in creating their new sorts, amazed with their imagination. Besides these, in some covered pavilions named after the Dutch royal family (Oranje Nassau, Beatrix, Willem-Alexander...) were displays of just as colourful orchids and lilies. I knew it: Holland is a country of flowers!

We drove from village to village and saw flower beds in front of every home, with beautiful arrangements of flowers. Every housing block had a flower garden outside. And of course, tulips always took pride of place! But if there was one thing that outnumbered the flowers, it was the cyclists. It felt as if everyone got around by bicycle - from men in business suits, to women in skirts and dresses, to schoolchildren, students and pensioners. Could Holland actually be a country of cyclists?

But no: Holland is a country of canals! Well-tended canals with boats, barges and even floating houses crisscross the country. A large part of its territory lies below sea level. In rural areas little houses with thatched roofs sit beside the canals, looking like the homes in fairytales where gnomes live. It seemed as if everything inside those homes had to be small - the windows, the doors, the furniture… but when I looked closer, it was an illusion: they were the same size as any other, and you could enter the house with no difficulty. And there was such space inside! I couldn't understand: how did they manage to turn a gnome's house into such spacious and cosy homes?

Utrecht

At last, we arrived in Utrecht, a small, spotless town, founded by the Romans in the 1st century, and nowadays home to many canals and cyclists. Narrow winding cobbled lanes, old churches with their bells peeling far and wide, fairytale little brick houses, ancient canals with humped bridges…

But the main reason for our journey was the auto market on the outskirts of Utrecht. As soon as our minibus came to a halt in the car park, my companions, with hungry looks in their eyes, went off in search of cars that fitted their tastes and budgets. I wasn't going to buy anything, but took a walk around the market all the same, looking at the cars, the salesmen and the buyers. I was interested in the people, not the automobiles.

By the evening all the men had bought a car, sorted out the paperwork, and had begun driving them back towards Lithuania to sell them on. For them, Holland was probably a country of cheap cars!

Vitas, a plump, greying old man, took me to an empty hangar at the edge of the market. There I stumbled upon some classic cars, the likes of which I had only heard about: Ford, Pontiac, Renault, Volvo, Citroen... A couple of dozen different cars from different eras were parked on the tarmac in the hangar, their chrome steel shining, like in a real car showroom. Some makes I had never heard of. It was like a museum! I looked at these cars in complete wonder. How much money would you need to maintain your own private classic car museum, and pay staff to look after them?

The owners of the hangar were two cheerful young men called Paul and Jan. Each of them had a glittering earring in their right ear. The familiar sight and smell of a *Maria Ivanovna* spliff in their mouths, mixed with the scent of expensive eau de cologne, created an intoxicating cloud around them. I asked them everything that interested me about their collection of cars, and they were only too happy to tell me about it. For my two new friends collecting and selling classic cars was both a hobby and a business. They bought old cars, renovated them, and then sold them on to collectors all over the world.

One of them, I think Paul, offered me a joint. I refused:

- No thank you. Medicine warns against drugs...
- But in Holland our medicine *is* drugs - replied Jan. - Doctors here prescribe cannabis to patients as pain relief and muscle relaxants.
- What pain could two healthy young men like you suffer from? - I answered back.
- We absorb the pain from this messed-up world of ours - said Paul, and they both burst out laughing.

I was used to getting attention from men, and was watching their reactions. But from their words and body language I could tell that they were interested in me not as a woman, but as a potential customer. They didn't hide their affection for one another, touching each other and calling each other by pet names. I realised that I was talking with a gay couple. Oh goodness, and what handsome men!

It was my first encounter with Dutch businessmen, and with Dutch gays. Now I was sure: Holland is a country of freedom!

Home in the minibus
Vitas and I went back to Klaidepa on our own. We talked for the whole 1,800km.

Vitas explained to me that in the Netherlands you could buy a good second-hand car for less than in Lithuania. German makes were the best, but Japanese weren't bad either. I had already begun to work this out myself, but he gave me the details and the prices. If you travel and pay the import taxes yourself, you could save 500 to 800 dollars.

Utrecht's auto market, it turned out, was the largest in Holland - and in fact the biggest in the whole of northern Europe. True, buying from there came with a risk. Sometimes stolen cars ended up there, before their owners had managed to inform the police, and every Tuesday in the big, enclosed hangar there was an open auction - but it isn't quite as simple as that. The cars go to auction 'right from the street', without an MOT or any servicing, with only their documents checked to avoid any disputes. The starting prices are about half of those found in showrooms, but grow as the bidding increases. Visitors need to be able to count in Dutch, so as to keep track of the prices being shouted out, and to raise their hands at the right time. Of course, it's possible to get your hands on a nice car for less than the going price. But you could also end up with an old taxi with an awful lot of miles on the clock.

- This Volkswagen we're sitting in now I bought at the auction last year - Vitas said, gently stroking it. - I was lucky. It isn't a bus, it's a greyhound! Look how she goes! - and he pressed the accelerator...

I wasn't really listening to him, but for some reason I have always remembered those cars.

The dark green Mercedes

The colonial legacy

Oh, my old Moskvich-412! It was the first car I ever fell in love with. I bought it with my ex-husband, almost-new. It was as red as the flag of the Soviet Union. We both hated that colour. But then we didn't have a choice – in those days you took what you were given. And compared to bumping around on minibuses and trams it felt like the best and most beautiful transport in the world. It wasn't a demanding car: she was happy to run on the cheapest A-66 petrol, and often helped us out in all sorts of situations. I felt as if she had a soul, and a personality. After a couple of years her motor began to make an unhealthy noise. We took her to be repaired, bought a new starter, put new caps on her wheels, and cleaned her until she sparkled. I looked at myself in those shiny hubcaps and was as happy as if I had bought some new Italian boots!

But as the saying goes, only Cognac gets better with age. The years went by, and our Moskvich fell apart in front of our eyes. Almost every week one thing or another would break. My mother would say to me:

- What do you need that old Soviet piece of junk for? Everyone is driving around in foreign cars now. Your uncle Yurgis brought an Opel back from Germany. Our neighbour Jonas has a Volkswagen...
- Mum, we're an independent country now. A Moskvich is a foreign car too!
- It's not a foreign car, it's a cursed legacy of colonialism! Urgh!

35

Was my mother right? Should I go and buy a proper European car? Could I afford one? And then I remembered what my acquaintance Vitas, the minibus driver, had told me about the auto market in Utrecht. I mulled it over. From a financial point of view, it was certainly tempting. Maybe the ends would justify the means? And if I was honest with myself, I had had enough of our red "colonial legacy".

The dark green Mercedes
After finding out from Vitas when he would be taking his next group of speculators to Utrecht, I arrived at the meeting place.

- Vitas, hi!
- Hello there! So you've decided to become one of us?
- Yeah, it's time I got myself a foreign car. Let's go!

And so our minibus, loaded with young men travelling to buy cars to resell, set off west: Lithuania - Russia - Poland - Germany - the Netherlands.

The final motorway, the Dutch *snelweg* A1, was a familiar sight. We turned left at a huge junction in Amersfoort, and early that morning we were in Utrecht. Being among the first to arrive, we waited, poised like bloodhounds, for the market to open. Then we scattered in search of cheap cars. The early bird catches the worm, and this meant that the best cars were ours to find! I spent a long time walking between them, losing myself in the commotion and scared that my inexperience would cause me to make a mistake. Wide-eyed at the selection of cars, I wanted to buy the shiniest and most beautiful. I wasn't thinking about the motor, the miles on the clock, the size of the tyres, about the fuel efficiency... There were just a lot of handsome cars - but their prices left me despondently squeezing my handbag with three thousand dollars inside. Finally, exhausted from traipsing through the market, I went back to see a 1985 dark green Mercedes. I had noticed her at the start, a model C-180 with an elegant body and cream-coloured upholstery. I had walked around her several more times, but I didn't have enough money to buy her. Her owner, a Dutch lady of a similar age to me, noticed me circling the car with a pained expression on my face. She spoke German, so we started talking. I told her about myself, and she told me that her husband had bought the car, that she had taken her children to nursery and school in it, but hadn't really driven it much. I summoned Vitas, who looked at the motor, the bodywork and the wheel arches, and then whispered to me that although this 'Merc' was getting on in years, it was still in excellent condition. The market was almost empty by now. The lady, knowing that no-one else was going to buy her car today, lowered the price. I let out a big sigh of relief, and we completed the deal. My fellow travellers, the men who were here to buy cars to resell, had long since made their own purchases and were already on their way back to Lithuania. For them time was money, and no-one wanted to wait for - or even be seen with - the woman with her head in the clouds, who hadn't chosen a car yet, and, for all they knew, might never find one that catches her fancy.

I had agreed with Vitas that if I were to buy something, we would travel back together. I didn't know the routes home, especially the way out of Utrecht, with its narrow and bendy streets, so I really wanted him to go in front of me in his Volkswagen bus. It was safer that way, too. We had all heard about Polish racketeers and Russian gangs on the roads, who stole money from the car dealers, and could even take their cars as well.

Vitas told me where to meet him, at a bus stop at the exit out of the town, and went away to take care of his own matters. I left my bag and other things in his minibus, and went to fill up the Merc with petrol, and to buy some food from a shop.

I arrived early at exit A28 to the *snelweg*. I waited for Vitas for an hour, then two. It was already getting dark. Then it started to rain, and he still didn't appear. Had he left without me? Had I turned up at the wrong stop? Mobile phones didn't exist yet, and there was no way of contacting him. I dusted myself off and decided: "I'm not a little girl, I'm not going to stand here and cry all night!", and took matters into my own hands.

The way home
I bought a map from a shop, and spent a long time running my finger over it, trying to work out the route I needed to take. I finally came up with a plan, and was on my way. I put the map right in front of me, on the steering wheel. I was sure I needed the *snelweg* A28, but for the life of me I couldn't find an exit to that cursed junction. I was in a new car, in a foreign country, with everything in a foreign language. My back was soaking with sweat, but I had nothing to change into – my bag was still in Vitas's bus. Finally, I found the way out - but soon after that, at the big junction in Amersfoort, I missed the turning on the right that would take me to the A1. I had to go around

three more junctions. My body was covered with sweat again. But in a constant nervous sweat, and with one finger pressed against my 'sat nav', I drove all night, until I reached the border between *Nederland* and *Deutschland*.

In Germany it got a bit easier. I was more or less familiar with the roads, and I had got used to driving the Mercedes. I could certainly feel the difference between it and the Moskvich: it didn't shake or veer to one side, and it didn't stall in the middle of the road. I felt more relaxed as I exited onto the Autobahn E30, folded my map away, and gently put my foot on the accelerator. As Vitas had said about his minibus: "She isn't a car, she's a greyhound – look how she goes!" I was going at 100… 120… 140… The seat began to vibrate, my heart was ready to burst out of my chest, and I could feel the velocity in every cell of my body. But even so, BMWs and Audis were still whistling past me, as if my Mercedes wasn't moving. This is what the Deutsche Autobahnen are like!

By the evening I was in Frankfurt an der Oder, where there is a border. On the other side is Poland – the most dangerous part of the journey. It was getting dark. I had been driving all night and all day, and now my tiredness was taking hold – my nose was almost touching the wheel. To make matters worse, it had started to rain. I got as far as a little Polish town, and spent the night in a motel.

In the morning I continued my journey.

Soon I began to notice groups of people parked in their cars by the roadside, and knew that they were racketeers. Seeing the Mercedes, the men in one car waved at me, ordering me to stop. But I looked straight ahead, and quietly and impudently drove past them. They took after me. In the rear mirror I saw a flash car catching me up fast. Oh God, what do I do? I decided that my most important possessions right then were my passport and money. I took them out of my purse and put them in my pocket. My pursuers were getting closer and closer. I panicked. When the car drew up alongside me, the men inside began to shout at me. To begin with they yelled in Polish:

- *Ktory rok? Ktory rok?*
- What?! I can't hear you! – I cried out, and gripped the wheel, desperately.
- Are you deaf? Or do you just have a death wish? – their leader screamed in Russian. - What year is that Merc?
- Seventy-nine... - I was so terrified the words barely came out of my mouth.

But those two words saved me! The bandits had no need for anything that old. Or maybe they didn't have the energy to deal with a woman who was playing deaf. Either way, the men began to back down, and then the car turned around entirely and drove back to where it had come from.

For hours I couldn't feel my body. It was as if I had been turned to stone. All I could do was whisper: "Thank you, God… Thank you, angels… Thank you, universe…"

I managed to regain my composure at the Russian border, where signs appeared ordering drivers to lower their speed.

For whatever reason I didn't come across any Russian bandits. But later, some experienced car dealers would tell me: you're always lucky your first time.

I arrived home alive, safe, and in the Mercedes. It turned out that Vitas arrived back a little earlier than I did; but he couldn't give my family any news about me. The way he told it, he had waited for me at our meeting place, but then gave up waiting, thinking that I had left without him. I pointed on the map to where I had been waiting. He showed me where he had been. Of course, we had been at different bus stops!

Despite my mistake, I was beaming with pride. I felt like a real used car dealer; I had made a deal just as good as any of the men I had travelled with. But I thanked God and all His angels for keeping me safe during my adventures on the roads. I told my mother, the rest of my family and my friends about my 'sat nav', about going at 180 km / hour on the German Autobahn, and about the Polish gang: how I had held my nerve, not stopping for them and refusing to give them my Mercedes. Everyone listened, their jaws almost touching the floor. My mother held me in her arms with tears in her eyes, and cursed all foreign cars...

I came to love my dark green Mercedes even more. She was actually older than our old red Moskvich, but in spirit she was much younger. It must be the Deutsche Qualitat! I took good care of her, bought a Karcher washer for her and always washed her myself, and only ever put A-93 petrol in her. And the German car treated her Lithuanian owner just as well. She never broke down, never misbehaved, never refused to go shopping, and always

patiently waited for me in car parks. We lived happily
ever after. And I have loved Mercedes ever since.

A warm autumn in Paris

I came home to Birmingham from Moscow with a whirl-wind of emotions inside me. I was still on a high when another adventure came calling...

Six months earlier my husband and I had made plans to spend a few days in Paris. We wanted to arrive near the end of September, because we had been told that in the autumn Paris is at her most beautiful. We had already booked our tickets and hotel.

Day One

And so, on 19 September we flew into Charles de Gaulle airport. Bienvenue en France!

Paris met us with warm sunshine. The city seemed happy and serene. But where was autumn? Was it always sum-mer in the city of lovers?

At the R. Kipling Hotel on Rue Blanche we were greeted like old friends. I had already stayed there once, in this old French house with six floors, and its entrance painted orange. I liked how warm and homely it felt, as well as the nice people who worked there. We were met by a handsome young Asian man, who spoke English. The three of us barely squeezed into the tiny old-fashioned lift. But this was Paris, after all: a tiny lift, a tiny room, tiny cafes - but with (as they say) softer mattresses, wider beds, softer duvets, fluffier pillows and silkier sheets than anywhere else. I had spent time in France's capital in the spring, in the summer, and now in the autumn. I have to say that the beds and blankets are the same as everywhere - but the city really does have its own special charm.

We unpacked our suitcases, changed into new clothes, and stepped out onto Rue Blanche. This narrow little one-way street leads to Place Blanche and Boulevard de Clichy, home of the famous Moulin Rouge. We went down into the metro and travelled to the no-less famous Galeries Lafayette.

Galeries Lafayette is a French chain of department stores with branches all over the world, but its flagship store for a hundred years has been on Boulevard Osman. The grandiose building is one of the city's historical monuments, as well as being one of the world's most expensive malls, and a Mecca for French shoppers.

And so, we walked into this historical monument. Looking up at the great glass cupola, the galleries with balconies and the glass bridge took our breath away. It was very beautiful, stylish, fashionable, as if the boutiques had been made from the delectable French pastries sold in all the Parisian boulangeries. All around were stores of the world's biggest brands, and expensive cafes and restaurants. In the centre of the main hall was a fabulous podium, where on Fridays there are always fashion shows to present the latest collections for sale in the mall. I heard that G.U.M in Moscow was built as a copy of Galeries Lafayette. But I was surprised by something else.

Everywhere, in addition to signs in French, there was writing in Chinese, and the assistants in the boutiques were of Asian descent: Chinese, Korean, Filipino, as well as Arab. There were so many wealthy shoppers from Asian countries that I would say they made up the majority.

Strolling through the mall, we went up to the seventh - top - floor. Right on the roof there is a restaurant, with a viewing platform with a view of the Eiffel Tower and all of Paris. What an incredible view! I then went along the Glasswalk – the glass bridge that links the parades of boutiques. For safety reasons only a few people are allowed to walk over at one time, so I had to wait in a queue. It is a long way up - and I have been afraid of heights all my life. It made me very queasy to look beneath my feet, but I overcame my fear, walked along the glass tiles, reached the end and took some photographs. Voila! It was an unforgettable feeling to not let my fears get the better of me.

After Galeries Lafayette, in the afternoon we went to the Louvre. As always, at the world-famous museum there was a huge queue, so we made do with a walk around the square, then from the banks of the River Seine we walked to the Jardin des Tuileries, opposite the Place de la Concorde. It is an idyllic place to take a stroll, and relax in the fresh air. We sat by a little pond, admired the sculptures and fountains, walked along the alleys, and decided that that was enough for one day.

Day Two
The next day we went to Versailles – the former residence of France's royalty, and now a suburb of Paris. On an autumnal September day the weather was glorious, as though the warmth of summer would never end. For us, coming from England with its damp autumns, it was almost too hot.

This excursion gave me particularly strong impressions and emotions. With its classical architecture and gardens

45

designed as pieces of art, Versailles truly is a place fit for kings and queens. Delicate paths, gorgeous fountains, colourful flowers, manicured trees and hedges; in some places, the leaves had just begun to turn yellow, giving them an autumnal feel. We wanted to take photographs of ourselves at every step. I was stunned by the majesty of the palace, and how enormous its grounds were. It would take several days to walk around all the royal apartments and salons. We galloped around to see as much in one day as possible...

In the evening, when we got back to our hotel, I just collapsed from tiredness and from the heat. I couldn't even think about a night-time walk-through Paris. We left that for the next day.

Day Three
Our day began with a visit to one of Paris's main sights, the beautiful snow-white basilica of Sacre Coeur. She sits proudly atop Montmartre, the highest spot in Paris, with a many-layered staircase of 237 steps leading up to her. Not without difficulty we made it to the top, and as our reward were treated to a magnificent panoramic view of Paris. Montmartre hill is a wonderful place to see the beautiful French capital in all its glory.

The basilica itself is stunning, too. The sculptures and large cupola are very impressive, while inside, underneath the cupola, is the Mosaic of Christ in Glory - a monumental mosaic that is the largest in Paris, and one of the biggest in the world. The famous organ of Sacre Coeur is also one of the biggest and oldest in the world.

Having taken the 237 steps down again, we walked for a while through the streets beneath Montmartre, and then went to see another of Paris's sights - the Centre Pompidou, the gallery for contemporary visual art.

We stopped at each of its floors and halls, amazed by how some of the modern artists see the world. The standout gallery at the Centre is the one dedicated to 20th century avant-garde pieces. I can't say that I am a fan of the primitiveness of the paintings and installations, but they do have something to them. I don't understand why people sit for hours looking at a green square or a purple rectangle - I prefer images that are more comprehensible. But I was impressed by paintings by the celebrated artists: Picasso, Christian Schad, Francis Picabia and Otto Dix, as well as Andy Warhol's portrait of Elizabeth Taylor. I noticed that the most important theme in works by artists at that time was a love of the female body. It wasn't important whether the woman was fat or thin: the naked body is a source of inspiration. But the most charming sight at the Centre Pompidou came from the viewing platform on the top floor: of Paris, the Seine, and the snow-white cupola of the Sacre Coeur Basilica ruling the skyline.

We also wanted to visit Place Charles de Gaulle, with its famous Arc de Triomphe. But we decided to have something to eat beforehand. In a cosy little café, they brought us some wonderfully soft, thick French crêpes. Some were crêpes Suzette, with an orange filling, and some were crêpes soufflées, with candied cherries... But straight after lunch I suddenly felt very tired, and started to feel pain in my back. My mood disappeared, as well as my desire to see the Arc. We decided not to go; it would be better to rest in the hotel for a little while, and then end the day with a walk-through Paris at night.

In the evening, as we left the hotel and stepped onto Rue Blanche, we saw a minibus with armed policemen parked in one corner. We hadn't noticed them before. We were taken aback, but thought it might have something to do with the area's reputation as a 'red light district'. Boulevard de Clichy, a little way past the legendary Moulin Rouge on Place Pigalle, was lit up with illuminations from nightclubs, peep shows, sex shops, and a building with a sign saying "Sexsodrom". The surrounding streets and squares were filled with suspicious-looking young men; outside the sex shops, young Parisian girls were standing in mini-skirts and high heels... And as if to confirm our suspicions, soon a black French man approached my husband and offered us some joints. Now there was a surprise! I remembered that this happens in Amsterdam... but Paris?? But yes, the world is becoming globalised - everywhere there are tourists, everywhere there are those 'red lights', and everywhere tourists are offered the same things...

When we went home to England and saw the news, I understood why I had felt that sudden tiredness and aches in my back. They had been warnings from above. Some of the strange moments during our night-time walk hadn't been strange at all, but necessary measures by the authorities to keep the city safe.

That night, after walking on Boulevard de Clichy and seeing the sex and drugs side of Paris, we went to a restaurant for dinner. Can you guess what we ordered?

Yes, of course: frogs' legs, a famous staple of French cuisine. The waiter told us that the chefs use the frogs' thighs: the meatiest and juiciest parts of their bodies.

- Ok, then bring us a fricassee of frogs' thighs, - I said.
- And which wine will madame et monsieur be drinking?

My husband thought for a while, ran his finger down the wine list, and ordered a Riesling from Alsace.

- An excellent choice, monsieur, - said the waiter, and walked elegantly back to the kitchen.

They say that the taste of frogs' legs is similar to chicken. I wouldn't say so. It has its own particular flavour...

Day Four

After breakfast on the last day of our trip, we went again to the square close to our hotel. We couldn't believe our eyes! In the very same place where the night before had been prostitutes and pimps, and where we had been openly offered drugs, now a fancy flea market had appeared! Antique furniture and crockery, vintage clothing and jewelry, paintings, dolls, books... The only reminders of the night before were a few Parisian men sleeping on benches, and an abandoned scooter on a pavement.

Before we left, we managed to take a ride on a cute little open-topped sightseeing tram. While French music played, a tour guide told us about all of Paris's sights... Unfortunately, the road up to Montmartre and the basilica of Sacre Coeur was closed off by the police, and the tram had to bypass it. We thought there must have been some kind of celebration happening that day.

And so, it was time to go home. At the hotel we waited for our taxi to the airport. But then came some unpleasant surprises, which reminded me of what had happened on my journey to Moscow. First, we got a text message to say that our driver would be 20 minutes late. We waited patiently. A few minutes later, someone from the taxi company called:

- All the streets in the centre of the city are blocked. Your taxi is stuck in traffic, nothing is moving. You would be better off getting a train to the airport.

We were calm about this - these things can happen when there are public holidays. No-one at the hotel had told us about any problems: everyone gave us a warm farewell, and we calmly set off for the train station.

On the platform at the station there was more trouble. Our train arrived, but the guard who checked our tickets didn't let us get on.

- What's the problem? How do we get to the airport?

He said something we couldn't understand, and waved his hand towards another platform.

I have to say that French people either don't speak English very well, or don't speak it at all. I found a girl in a yellow tabard who, mercifully, did speak English. It transpired that this way to the airport was also closed. We had to get on a different train, get off at the next station, and then get on a bus (at bus stop B3).

Something had happened in Paris, and it certainly wasn't a celebration. I became very anxious. Whether in Moscow or Paris, these transport nightmares were following me around like a stray dog. But of course, we weren't the only ones trying to get to the airport, and so we all did as we were told.

We got off the train at the next station, and there every 20 meres there was a member of staff showing the passengers where to go. At the turnings there was someone with a megaphone shouting directions, and answering questions, but in French. We stumbled along in the sweaty crowd. Along the street that led towards the bus stop, directions had been marked in dark blue on the pavement. There were members of staff here too, pointing the way. Wow! The French have a lot of experience in taking care of people's safety. But still, my anxiety was getting even stronger. Are we going to make it to our flight, or not?

When at the bus stop an African man in a yellow tabard tried to take my suitcase, I didn't want to give it to him. But he laughed, said something in French, and made a gesture to show that he was only going to put it on the bus for me. The bus driver was a black woman with a million dreadlocks in her hair. She said hello to everyone as they got on, and gave us all a smile. In front of us was a Russian family. The woman and her daughter calmly got on to the bus and sat down in some seats, but when the man got on, he stood frozen in front of the driver:

- Madame?!

The woman laughed, and said:

- Oui, oui! Madame!

We laughed too. The man finally moved, and we got onto the bus. Are Russian men really so surprised when bus drivers are madames?

The bus got us to the airport surprisingly quickly. We managed to catch our flight, and landed safely in Birmingham. It was only when a friend called me that I realised that Paris was burning for more reasons than just the weather. I read the news on the internet, and thanked God, my guardian angels, my back, and much else besides, that we had not gone to the Arc de Triomphe that Saturday.

What I saw on the screen was like another French Revolution. Pogroms on its streets; smashed windows; places on fire; barricades: new scenes like those in the painting by Eugène Delacroix, 'Liberty Leading the People'. Men were running bare-chested on the Champs-Élysées. The police had to use tear gas. Hundreds of people had been arrested, and some had died.

I read about what had caused the unrest. On 21 September a movement called the Yellow Vests had organised a demonstration to protest about global warming and environmental damage. I couldn't get my head around it. How were they going to stop global warming with weapons, fires and fights?

This was my autumn in Paris. A city of museums and artists, of Asian Parisians and African Parisians, of exquisite food and love for sale - and a city of barricades and blocked streets.

The girl who writes

(Some notes about boys and girls who write)

Winning an award from the Eurasian Creative Union - and presenting my book *Nurse, give me a pill for death* in Moscow - whetted my literary appetite. I began to think of myself as a writer, and entered the book into the Eurasian Creative Guild's literary competition, "Open Eurasia".

Of course, I wasn't hoping for much: I sent the application form and forgot about it. The next thing I knew, I was looking at the title of my book in the competition's shortlist. Had they really noticed me? Do I really need to go to Brussels for a literary festival?!

There was only one answer to all these questions: Yes!

And so in November 2019, on a flight from Birmingham to Brussels via Frankfurt, I arrived at Zaventem airport. I was met with a big billboard:

"Welkom in Vlaanderen en Brussel!"

Seeing as I was a nominee in the Open Eurasian Literature Festival and Book Forum, and as I had come to the capital of Europe, why not stay in the very building of the European Commission... The four-star Charlemagne Hotel on Boulevard Charlemagne was an excellent choice – comfortable and modern. But the name confused me. What was a Charlemagne? Ah, they mean the German king, Karl. What a language the French have!

From my room on the top floor, the ninth, there was a wonderful view of the city. Every morning, looking out of my window at the gothic spires of the Grand Place in the distance, I said: "Bonjour, Brussels!" And looking to the left at the enormous building of the European Commission, at the limousines chauffeuring their dignitaries and the armed guards protecting them, I said "*Privet*, Capital of Europe!" And then, still with a little hope in my heart, I thought: "Maybe Brexit won't really happen after all?"

At the literary festival I tried to take part in all the compulsory events. There were quite a few of them. But at the same time, I wanted to see the city. I had to mix business with pleasure. I got up very early and walked around Brussels' little streets, and then did the same in the lunch breaks, and after the meetings were over. I liked the buildings decorated with columns, sculptures and other details, so the chapel to Scientology on Boulevard de Waterloo - where all our events took place - left an impression on me. And the Royal Castle in the Royal Greenhouses was very beautiful. The castle is a copy of the Palais de Luxemborg in Paris. And how could I not mention Brussels' famous Atomium? The structure is designed in the form of an iron crystal, magnified 165 billion times. Inside there is a system of lifts and walkways from one part of the atom to another, and inside each one there are various exhibitions. The outside is built from stainless-steel plates. It is an ingenious and unique symbol of Brussels, and on clear days it dazzles the eyes with its reflections of the sun. In some ways it is just like the Eiffel Tower.

In the centre of Brussels modern buildings go side by side with gothic ones, creating an organic combination of styles: Renaissance, Flemish baroque and Roman. Some districts reminded me of Amsterdam, which I knew well (although I didn't go to Brussels' 'red light district', or partake in any joints). I walked through the narrow streets in the centre of the city, and took lots of photographs.

One day I came across the shop of the famous Belgian chocolate company Neuhaus Chocolates. What luxuriant window dressings! How beautiful, stylish and original everything looked! Behind the glass there was Neuhaus' very own chocolate, caramels, waffles, truffles, pralines, roasted candied nuts, muesli… it all made my mouth water. I wanted to buy the lot! Then I found the famous bronze "Peeing Boy" statue - a little fountain on the corner of a building, cordoned off and surrounded by a crowd of tourists. I wish there could have been a "Peeing Girl" as well. There was no time to see any more of Brussels' sights, or any of its museums.

My attention turned back to the writers. I liked absolutely everyone I met. I met and spoke with some very interesting fellow participants, from various parts of Eurasia: Nastya Kuzmicheva (Belarus), Aya Maksutova (Kazakhstan), Aleksandra Taan (St. Petersburg), Oksana Zhukova (Crimea), Lyudmila Dubovetskaya (Moldova), and many others.

On one of the days, I was approached by the Guild's ambassador from Kyrgyzstan, Gulnar Emil. She said something to me and looked me deeply in the eyes. Then suddenly she began to recite one of her poems:

Your eyes, your eyes.
Oh, those light blue eyes…

Sadly, I don't remember the rest. I remember that I opened my eyes wider, and was incredibly surprised by such an upfront show of affection.

Many people showed an interest in *Nurse, give me a pill for death*. The topic of helping people who are sick strikes a chord with people, and I was happy to give some advice, or just speak to guests who had found themselves in similar difficult situations. People told me their own stories, and shared their pain with me. Oksana Zhukova from Crimea shared a lot with me about herself, and her elderly mother.

All the festival participants spoke with each other, and swapped books and addresses. On the first day the vice-president of the Guild himself, Marat Akhmedjanov, gallantly helped me to find my place. I found myself at the same table as a small Tatar man from St. Petersburg, who turned out to be both a very reputed writer and the editor of a printed magazine. He was caring and extremely courteous, and when I asked him for his address, meaning his email address, he gave me his home address.

- Are you inviting me to visit you? – I joked.
- Well why not! – answered Gumer Karimov.

I was absolutely overjoyed.

Oksana introduced me to a Kazakh man, from Almaty. At the time I didn't even remember his name. Later, at the presentation of Stephen Bland's book about his travels in

Central Asia, he asked several awkward questions that made the author feel uncomfortable. "What a mean man!" - I thought at the time. On top of it all he was a professor of physics and mathematics. "I'm not going to get into any debates with that Marat Uali!" - I decided.

And so arrived the long-awaited announcement of the prize-winners.

After a delicious dinner with red wine, which we were free to pour ourselves from a big decanter at a separate table, the ceremony to announce the winners of each category began. Compere Marat Akhmedjanov called out the names, and to hearty applause the winning authors were presented with certificates. Ion Jani... Ekaterina Khlebnikova... Sagynbubu Berkenaliyeva... Nadezhda Serebrennikova... We were all happy for our peers, clapping and congratulating each other. Finally, we got to the category 'Best work by a female author'. I started to get nervous: I couldn't win, could I? Marat Akhmedjanov announced slowly and dramatically: "And the winner is... Zhanna Golubitskaya!" And that was that: my hopes had drowned, as if in the fountain of the peeing boy. I took a deep breath and calmed down... and then I heard my name:

- And in second place... *"Nurse, give me a pill for death"* by Aldona Grupas!

Oh my God! I was hearing loud bells ringing, accompanied by drums and fanfare! When I heard my surname, I almost passed out. It was such a shock - this couldn't be happening! Was there another Aldona Grupas here?

I walked to the stage as if in a dream. But as I received my certificate, I composed myself, and thanked everyone for putting my humble work in such high esteem. When I got back to my seat, my friends began to congratulate me and take photos of me. They were truly happy for me. I still couldn't quite come to my senses. I couldn't believe that this had all happened, and I had won a prize in a literary competition. Had I really become a writer? It was true. Oh my God, it has happened!

But all good things come to an end. The festival came to a close, and it was time to say goodbye. Gagik Ogadjenyan and Ravil Abdulov, having read my book, remembered my husband's name and asked me to send him their regards. Everyone embraced each other, and kissed each other goodbye like family... And I, looking for the last time from the window of my room at the Charlemagne, waved at Brussels and said "See you again, boys and girls who write!"

And then Zaventem airport, and a last look at Belgium from the plane... Adieu, Brussels!

There was another connecting flight in Frankfurt. I had some time before my flight to Birmingham, so I made myself comfortable in the airport cafe. I got myself a coffee, called a Russian friend of mine, and began to tell her all about my trip. And only then did it really dawn on me. My voice was trembling as I told her that I had won a prize, and they had given me a certificate:

-   Galina, can you imagine, in Brussels I really became a writer!

There were tears in my eyes, but they were tears of joy. The girl in me who writes was so worried, but was now so happy.

My way to Reiki

Situations

In 1989 I started working at the resort town of Palanga in Lithuania, practising underwater massage. We worked six days a week, and it wasn't easy. Our hands were in the water almost all the time, where many chemicals were used to disinfect the baths. To treat our hands we were given alcohol that was no lower than 96% proof, so one day when I was there, a funny situation occurred. I was massaging a client—a middle-aged man – when the head nurse came and brought out the alcohol. You had to sign some papers before they gave it to you, so I apologised to the client and stepped aside. When I returned, the man looked at me with a smile and asked:

'What did they give you?' 'Alcohol,' I replied.

'They give you that to keep your spirits up?' he asked. Well, he got me laughing, but I explained they give us alcohol to disinfect our hands. He almost jumped out of the bath in shock.

'You pour such goodness onto your palms?!'

He was quite upset. Everyone has their own taste, of course.

Colleagues

Most of the staff were quite young. We enjoyed working together and even spending some of our free time just hanging out. Those were the best bits of those years, celebrating birthdays and visiting one another as much as we could.

Palanga is a town by the sea; it is very beautiful, with a large park, pedestrianised zones and cycle paths. The city is fresh and calm, with an air like the waves lapping the shore. During the winter it's pretty empty, though, and you'll only ever meet locals or people who've come to receive treatments at a sanatorium.

In the summer, the face of the town changes and it becomes somewhat of a 'tourist anthill.' There are throngs of people visiting the numerous cafés and restaurants which cater to all tastes. The main street leading to the sea is a favourite spot for evening walks - something is always happening there, and the street vendors offer everything from souvenirs and clothing to smoked fish. Restaurants endeavour to attract customers, not only with their exquisite menus but also with performances from local pop stars, so, naturally, loud music spills from all around. Sometimes there are various charity fairs with presentations and sports events. The city offers all sorts of fun entertainment, and for those who just want to relax in silence, they can drive out to the outskirts and find peace in moments.

In the summer, the golden beaches of Palanga are always filled with people. The bridge to the sea is the most visited spot. Overlooking the majestic Baltic Sea, it seems to pride itself on its popularity. All you have to do is hope for good weather.

The season opening ceremony takes place on the last weekend of May and is usually very well organised. People from all over the world come to see it, and it's interesting to talk to some of them as you always end up learning something new. We would chat with the newcomers as we would amongst ourselves, talking about everything from politics and philosophy to everyday problems.

Our memories from this time ensure we are friends to this day.

A New Take on the World

During my time working in Palanga, a psychotherapist by the name of Anatoly Kashpirovsky was becoming very popular. He performed mass hypnosis and healing sessions and would always be on the television. His appearances were watched by huge audiences, and he claimed to have healed at least ten million people. His appearances were discussed with fervour and he was the sensation of the time.

Then, word started spreading about a healer with a similar practice called Juna. It was rumoured almost all the country's top leaders took treatment sessions with her. I thought to myself: "So many unusual things have suddenly started to come to light. I wonder what else is there that we haven't heard of yet?" I was very interested in Juna's practice, but I didn't know enough about it. "Maybe it's some kind of mysticism," I thought. One day, I came across an advertisement in the newspaper which stated that a masseuse teaching non-contact massage in accordance with Juna's practice was visiting. I didn't really understand the concept of contactless massage - how could there possibly be a massage without contact with the body? - but, on the advice of a friend, I signed up for these courses.

During the class, I devoured every word as she told us about Juna and her method of healing people with the energies that surround our bodies. All of these previously incomprehensible concepts were so interesting to me. Nobody had spoken about bio-energy before, and nobody had ever taught us anything like this at school. It was here that I first learnt that there are psychic 'vampires' who 'drain' energy from other people in order to 'feed,' and a person from whom this energy has been 'pumped out' feels 'like a squeezed lemon.' This chimed with me because I had experienced things like that before; moments when I felt somehow wrong and exhausted. I had never thought it had anything to do with having the energy pumped out of me, though.

It was very strange for me to hear all this, but I became interested in this new information. Once, after a lecture, I even asked a friend:

- Diana, do you have any idea what they are talking about here? Am I stupid, or is the lecturer stupid?

We laughed at these lectures, but continued to attend them because, of course, our curiosity took over. The longer we practised as masseuses, however, the more we realised that our techniques were far from perfect.

The turn of the decade brought many changes. There were rumours that hospitals and sanatoriums would be closed, and the staff would no longer be needed. I quit my job, and the hospital where I used to work was converted into a spa hotel. The lack of work wasn't easy, so I always had my eyes peeled for advertisements in the newspapers. During that off-time, I attended yoga classes, meditated, and began to improve not just my body, but also my soul.

The Beginning

One day, I read an announcement in a newspaper that a doctor and his team from Moscow were coming to our city to run a course in non-contact massage in accordance with Juna's practices. Since I was already somewhat familiar with the concept, although I had not yet fully understood the essence of the procedure, I was instantly fascinated. The courses had to be paid for, though, and during those times it was a lot of money. I didn't have that kind of cash, but I was saved by my mother, who really believed in me. She gave me the money and told me to go and study these methods and practices.

She was so right! Ah, mothers! How do you always know what your kids need the most?

Juna's Methods

The training lasted for about a month. There were around thirty of us, among us doctors, massage therapists and nurses, and we received theoretical knowledge and explanations as to how, what and why. Every single day I spent on the course was a revelation, and I felt I was improving my techniques by leaps and bounds. We were taught how to feel our own energy and the energy of others. We were taught how to diagnose others correctly, identifying the 'gaps' in human energy, and all this without touching the body.

Our teachers also held several events at a local concert hall, where they showed their mastery of hypnosis. Volunteers were invited onto the stage, and several audience members agreed to be put under. The hypnotist put these people under, and they performed his tasks. After being released from his influence, they did not remember what they had done, and when they were told, they were surprised and laughed.

When I first saw hypnosis with my own eyes, I didn't like it. What I experienced shocked and frightened me. I didn't like that the hypnotist was able to control people, and I thought it wasn't safe. My emotions were all over the place, swinging between surprise and disbelief. I must confess that I could hardly bear these shows. For some reason, anger boiled within me. When I left the first show, I thought these methods did everything but heal the person, and every time I tried to calm down, I just got angrier.

When we took the exam, the teachers said that some of our colleagues would not be able to practice this method because they did not have the energy they needed. I turned out to be one of the lucky ones, though, and I passed the non-contact massage exam and was told I could use this method to help people.

The methodologies were based on focus and feelings. We had to feel and understand what the person in front of us feels. These methodologies later became the guiding light for the rest of my life. I have used them in my work almost all the time, whilst continuing to develop and try other things.

The First Steps
Upon receiving my diploma in non-contact massage, I went to my mother's house to share my joy with her, and,

of course, I made her my very first patient. I did everything according to the methodology we were taught, focusing partly on my energy and partly on the notes I had written. My mother immediately said she felt something like waves moving through her body. She liked what I was doing and invited her friend over to experience the procedure.

My mother's friend had been feeling bad for some time. Her stomach ached and it wouldn't go away. She had been to the doctors on numerous occasions, but they couldn't pin-point what was wrong, so when my mother told her what I'd learnt, she happily agreed to the procedure.

Within a few minutes of my starting to pass my hands over her body, the woman suddenly began to cry. Tears rolled down her cheeks, and I became scared and asked if I'd done something wrong. I was still very inexperienced, but we had been taught that this method shouldn't be able to harm a person.

The woman apologised for scaring me and said: 'Everything is alright; I just had to cry. Your treatment helped me a lot. I feel much better; my stomach is calmer and doesn't hurt anymore.'

I was surprised, and I had a lot of questions. What had I done? Why were the pains gone? Why was the woman crying? I still couldn't completely believe I could help anyone with this method, and so I asked my mother:

-   Mum, am I a witch?

She laughed.

- 'No, you're not a witch,' she replied. 'Apparently, you have a gift from God for healing people.'

Supernatural
Prior to that day, the concept of miracles did not exist in my life. I never knew I had such 'supernatural' abilities, for there was nothing which had given them to me: lightning hadn't struck me, and I hadn't drowned in a well and come back to life... That is to say, there were no external triggers. It was my own curiosity that had led me to discover my 'energy' and the concept of non-contact treatment.

This first session was the beginning of a new path I had set for myself. My 'miracles' were promoted through word of mouth, and people were soon coming to my house to ask for help. After each session I gained more and more confidence. I helped people with various diseases and was invited by a group of women from the district to perform non-contact massage for several women there. One of them underwent my sessions with great distrust, and I remember her saying:

- You really are helping me, yet I just don't believe in your treatments.

I replied that all that matters was the outcome, regardless of what you might believe. After all, I'm not a saint, and I don't need anyone to believe in me.

I continued doing what I had been taught. I kept statistics, made observations, and wrote them in my diary. I realised that each body is unique, but was able to group some symptoms according to certain criteria, so I knew how to work in similar situations.

Feelings

Every person on this Earth is different, and each has their own energy. Some feel the workings of my treatments, others do not, but they all see the changes it makes. Of course, my feelings also play a very important role in the process.

When I work, I can feel the person's problems and troubles at the tips of my fingers, be they pain, a scar, or something else. As I gained experience, I gradually began to implement my own methods into my work. Even though each case is different, the framework has always been and will remain the same. With this in mind, let me tell you a story of how I met a certain woman who, in my opinion, has determined my destiny for the rest of my life.

A Way

An elderly woman from our city who lived with her granddaughter found out about me from a mutual friend, and called to talk about her problems. There were the usual complaints: joints, backache, etc., but her main goal was different: she wanted to talk about her great-grand-children. They were two boys, six and seven-years-old who had food allergies; they could not eat mayonnaise, eggs and some other foods. This was new to me, as up until now I had not worked with people with allergies.

I answered her honestly, saying I couldn't promise anything because I didn't know whether it would be successful, but I agreed to try to help them. And so I set to work.

For ten days, both boys were treated to thirty-minute sessions. It wasn't easy: the boys laughed and made faces at each other. Whilst I was working with them, I also had sessions with their grandmother. When I finished the treatments, we said goodbye and parted ways.

The Turning Point
A couple of weeks after the New Year which saw in 1991, I received an unexpected call. During that time we lived in a communal apartment block, so everyone knew everyone else's phone number. The operator said they were calling me from Germany. I thought: "Calling me from Germany? Perhaps this is some kind of mistake? I don't know anyone in Germany."

Still, I stayed on the phone and greeted them, and a woman with a pleasant introduced herself as Walli, and said I had once treated two boys and their grandmother. Of course, I remembered this family. Walli thanked me for healing the children, and so I realised I had the ability to help people with their allergies, or at the very least to lessen their symptoms.

'Now they eat eggs and mayonnaise by the gallon,' Walli joked before asking: 'Could you perhaps come to Germany? We are very interested in your methods, and would like to try out the same sessions. Several people will be happy to welcome you here.'

Germany

This left me speechless. Germany? West Germany? How would I even get there? Lithuania had just regained its independence, but the border was still closed, and I would need a visa. I asked about it, but my interlocutor, it turned out, would arrange almost everything. She said she just needed to know my surname and place of residence, and she would make an invitation. She had also thought about how I would get there; her son-in-law would take me to Germany by car at the end of the month.

I had to apply for a visa in two weeks. A few days later, I received a letter from Germany with an invitation, so I had ten days to get the visa. I didn't know how to do it or where to go. At that time, I didn't have a computer, let alone the internet. After doing some digging, though, I knew I'd eventually find something, and so I did.

Challenges

I discovered we had a German representative office in the city and went there, but was disappointed to learn that it had shut down. It was a time of change; some things were just opening whilst others were closing, and the only German representative left was in Vilnius.

I was upset. The one opportunity I had to visit this foreign country I had only heard about in films and read about in books drifted away from me like a cloud. I called Walli's mother and told her my situation. She listened, reassured me and told me where I should go. She knew the process very well, since she went to Germany to visit her daughter every year.

Time for a Change
Walli's mother gave me the address of the German embassy in Vilnius, and so I went. By that time the embassy had moved, but there was a notice on the door with their new address, so I went there, finally checked in, and started waiting.

I had a hundred different thoughts flying through my head: "How am I going to talk to the people? I don't know German. Will they let me have a visa?" My fears were in vain, though. There was an interpreter at the embassy, and I was kindly received. They asked about the purpose of the visit, and I filled out a form. The one thing they stressed was that it would be better not to show these documents on the Russian-Lithuanian border; it was fine to do so at the Polish-German border, but only if they asked. And that was it: to my relief and with great happiness, I had a visa.

I returned home, and with joy in my heart, I start- ed packing my suitcase. Walli's daughter called me, and we agreed when they would pick me up.

The Borders
During the time in which I was arranging the visas, I talked with Walli's mother and grandmother a lot, and we became friends. They told me a lot about Germany, and about Walli herself. I was still nervous about the trip, however, because I didn't know these people very well. Shortly, though, for the first time in my life, I was to visit the mysterious "non-Soviet" Western world! Before that, I had only been to Poland. And so, at the end of January 1991, I set out on my journey not even suspecting how much it would change my life.

The Trip

We drove through Kaliningrad, and I successfully crossed the Lithuanian-Russian border with my Polish visa. No one knew exactly where I was going, and no one asked. Surprisingly, at the Polish-German border, no one even asked to see my documents. I had been frightened by the stories told by my acquaintances, but now the last barrier was behind me. I had officially made my first trip to the West.

Lights on the Road

It was a late winter evening as I sat in the back of the car heading to my destination. At one point, I saw a place on the highway completely illuminated. I was surprised. What was it; a circus? I had never seen a garland of so many lights on the road before. It turned out the lights marked off a lane which was under repair, and that this is done everywhere so drivers can see where to go. When I saw these lights for the first time, it really impressed me that something so bright could be just a normal occurrence.

This was my very first impression of being 'abroad' - those lights on the road.

We drove through East Germany for a long time before reaching West Germany. Finally, my goal was drawing close, but I was afraid of meeting everyone. My fears had returned once more: How will they greet me? What will they think of me?

I needn't have worried; I was met by wonderful people with whom I am still friends to this day. Moreover, they greeted me as if we had known each other for years. They were impressed that their grandchildren were now free of their allergies and talked about it constantly. Sure that their greeting was sincere and honest, I was finally able to relax.

Work
In Germany, much work awaited me, and many clients had already made appointments. Walli and I discussed all the nuances: where I would work and what I need to do so. So, I ended up having my own room where I lived, and a room where I worked and received clients.

Communication
As I couldn't speak German, it was difficult for me to communicate. Walli became my translator. When she went to work and there was no one to translate, however, communication was a constant problem. Little by little, I started writing down words and asking Walli what they meant. Gradually, I began to speak German. Then I began to study books and textbooks, and used German when working with clients. Although my language skills were still very bad, I began to be able to talk about what I needed.

The first thing I learnt to ask was: 'how are you feeling?' or 'what do you feel?'

I learnt the names of organs, ailments and diseases in German, including back pain, bronchitis, and heart disease. Even though I did not diagnose anyone, I said where (in which places) I felt changes in their energy.

A Certain Incident

I worked with the body by attempting to feel a lack of energy, or search for any place where a "special signal" arose. It could be a tingling in my fingers, a cold shudder down my spine, or a sudden pain which would pass through my arms or feeling as if I had suddenly caught a fever.

There was a case when one woman literally fainted during my session after I had put my hands on her back, near her kidneys. When she regained consciousness, I told her she should see a doctor and the sooner the better.

After a while, she came back and thanked me for the advice, saying she had kidney stones which she didn't know about before. She had felt bad once before and complained to a doctor about her pains, but they had found nothing. After my session, which ended very quickly, she went to another doctor - a private one this time. After performing the relevant tests, this doctor found her kidney stones. After this incident, I always took great care when working on people's backs.

Sessions

In all my years of working, I have had many other clients approach me with kidney problems, but no one else has ever fainted. People with kidney problems have reacted differently to my sessions: some were sweating or pale, others were suddenly drowsy. I followed the reactions of the clients carefully and knew when it was time to end the session. Basically, my sessions went like this: the client stood in front of me and I began to work, directing my hands towards their body, but avoiding contact at all costs; I "felt" their problems etched into their bodies. For example, it could be pain in a certain area, and I would feel tingling in my fingers, coldness, or heat. I have experienced many different sensations whilst working.

Allergy

What was unexpected for me was that I was able to help people get rid of their allergies.

Once I was approached by a patient with food allergies (like the boys). She couldn't eat fruits and vegetables. I agreed to conduct the course, but warned her I didn't know if my sessions would cure her. At the end of the course, she went on vacation at sea, promising to visit me upon her return to tell me how she was feeling. As I was constantly with clients, the weeks passed quickly, but eventually, as promised, the woman called and we agreed to meet. Walli and I were looking forward to it.

The bell rang, and Walli opened the door, greeted her, and immediately asked the question:

– Well, how is it?

The woman literally shone with happiness. She looked so well and refreshed. She hugged me with great joy and said:

'I didn't just eat fruits; I devoured them by the dozen!' She spoke without stopping. At first she had tasted one fruit, and once she saw that nothing was going to happen, she ate tons of them.

Talk about a miracle. She was indescribably happy and asked to do a few more sessions 'to consolidate.'

Method

Later, when meeting with specialists in the same field as me working on non-constant treatment and energies, I discussed the method itself with them. I wonder, where did it come from? After all, even Juna had to learn her methods somewhere.

One of my colleagues, a woman, told me about the philosophy behind Reiki. It was very similar to what I was doing, so I became interested, and decided to learn more about Reiki when I returned home.

Three weeks had passed, and it was time for me to go back. My clients asked me: 'When will you come again?' Since I didn't want to disappoint them, I promised to return next year. Walli said she would be happy to have me anytime I wanted.

This is how I started my career, and as a result I travelled to many countries over the course of the next thirteen years. Before that, though, when I returned from Germany, I felt uneasy. Everything was as normal at home, but it seemed terribly neglected, disorderly and ugly. I was in no mood to do anything. I felt like a fish washed ashore and lacking water.

Spiritual Practices

I started to become interested in the philosophy behind Reiki. My curiosity about this kind of knowledge pushed me forward. I was wondering: "Why are these things happening?" "Where does it come from?", and "How do you explain it?"

Gradually, I found like-minded people; it turned out there were a lot of them. It was a large community, but I had not known about it. I found books on Reiki in the city's bookstores, and the members of this community were happy to share their experiences and thoughts about this phenomenon. I found it all very interesting. We met, meditated, and shared our observations and experiences.

I want to tell everyone who does not know about the philosophy of Reiki exactly what it is, where it comes from, and what its purpose is.

When you perform spiritual practices, you first learn to become aware of your own powers. When you realise them, you realise how connected you are with the people who come into your life. Understanding this gives rise to a feeling of endless gratitude towards them, and towards life itself.

Reiki

What is Reiki? It is one of the original treatments in alternative medicine, a method first developed by Mikao Usui in early 19th century Japan. Reiki is the natural energy of health, and the power of Reiki is transmitted to students during initiations when the master-teacher activates the student's chakras to transmit Reiki energy through them. Mikao Usui claimed to have first learnt about Reiki in ancient Tibetan scriptures dating back to 2500 BC.

Reiki practitioners hold the patient's wrists with their fingers, like bracelets. Specialists receive Reiki energy directly from the universe, and during the session they become conductors of this energy. This energy is also called the 'life energy of the universe.' It harmonises and strengthens the functions of internal organs, removes toxins and chemicals, restores mental balance, helps to improve wellbeing, and cleanses the body as well as the mind.

The Five Principals
Mikao Usui recommended the following five spiritual principles which should be practiced:

I am without wrath
I am calm
I am thankful
I am honest
I love everyone around

He analysed his experiences and came up with these important tenets so that almost anyone can practice Reiki.

Subsequently, these rules became the most important philosophical concept in Reiki. They are:

Reiki brings health, happiness, and security. One cannot survive today without Reiki energy.

Do not harbour anger towards others or yourself. Respect parents, teachers and elders.

Earn your living.

Thank everyone for everything. Be attentive and kind to everyone.

Olga Potemkina: *The Miracle of Touch*
There are many different descriptions of Reiki today. I studied and followed the descriptions of 'Universal Life Energy.' This term best describes Reiki as a natural way to restore health.

The Natural Balance
We live in an energetic world that nourishes and satisfies all our vital needs. When the flow of energy does not change, we feel balanced. Therefore, the primary task of Reiki is to restore the natural balance of human energy. Reiki masters never diagnose their patients, for it is the doctor's job to do so. A Reiki master only works with human energy.

Steps
To become a Reiki Master or Teacher, special initiations are required. Once I received my first initiation, I realised I needed to go further. My first initiation opened the door for me to the philosophy of Reiki. I learnt from my

practice and from books that Reiki can be used as a universal and safe healing technique. From that point, it became clear to me exactly how I could help these people, for they were healing with me.

In theory, I believed Reiki could cure all diseases, but unfortunately, in practice, that was not the case. This led me to start looking for an answer. Why were the practices we were taught only partially successful? Why couldn't Reiki free every one of their problems?

Theory and Practice
Through practice I eventually realised why not everyone can be treated with Reiki. I first came across this information during one of my training sessions, when the doctors were discussing what kind of people could heal and what kind could not.

A Reiki Master is simply a channel that transfers energy to another person. The thing that's very important to consider when doing this is the personality of a person, their inner world, motivation and spiritual balance. The success of the method is only guaranteed if there is a pure and spiritual mutual trust between the Reiki master and the client.

Modern Reiki practice, like any "living" method, develops and finds its "talents." For me, Reiki is not only a healing process but also a path that leads to new achievements, new goals and a brand new, brighter future.

Dreams come true

I was born in Riga, Latvia, but I spent my summers at my grandmother's village in Lithuania. As a child, I dreamed about living in Lithuania too. I dreamed; I asked my parents; I begged my guardian angel – I prayed to God for my wishes to be fulfilled. And finally, that day came.

However, after many years in Lithuania, my life changed again. I had foreign friends and began to travel abroad, initially to Poland and then to Germany. When I travelled to West Germany, I was astounded by the differences between the two countries. Commuting annually to Germany to visit friends, I started to dream about life abroad. Friends gave me the idea that maybe I could go to live in Germany.

I was a trained nurse, having qualified back in 1979, and my husband was a doctor. I had worked as a medical sister, but the pay was poor, so I had gone into business, opening my own beauty salon. My husband and I knew that there was great demand for medical professionals in other countries, and the idea of living abroad appealed to us both. My husband liked Germany, but he refused to go there, largely because he couldn't speak the language. He said he would go only to English-speaking countries. So again, I began dreaming of going to another country – although I was not sure where that might be.

In 2005, I was a part-time law student at the Riga Law Institute of Klaipeda. Lectures were held four nights a week, with most of the students holding jobs on the side. After the lectures, I would often meet with colleagues in a popular café called Chilli Pizza. We discussed our work, our lives, and our futures.

I will never forget one meeting in particular. I was talking with Ula, a fourth-year student, about the uncertain future of the Institute and its qualifications, and how this left me and the other students in an ambiguous situation. At the time, there were rumours that Lithuania was considering not recognising our law diplomas, which would mean all our study would have been for nothing. You study, you learn, and you earn a diploma – and then it's not worth the paper it's printed on. What a shame! A lawyer without a diploma won't get anywhere.

However, I said that I was an optimist, and no matter what happened, I would be okay. After all, I was already a trained nurse.

I still, to this day, remember the surprised response of Ula.

"You're a nurse?" she said. "What are you doing here? You already have a good profession! Drive to England; they need nurses there. You will earn a good living!"

I was shaken by those words and the manner in which they were expressed. I had never imagined that I could just drive to England and find work. When I got home, I told my husband what my good friend had said. He was not at all surprised. He said that a friend of ours – another doctor – was using intermediaries in Lithuania to help him search for a job in the United Kingdom. He was attending English-language classes for doctors in Vilnius.

What a coincidence! I had been dreaming of working abroad, and now I had been told how to go about it. The answer had been handed to me on a silver platter.

My husband became infected with my fire and determination. Through his friend, we started making plans for him to find work as a doctor in England, contacting various organisations that provided the required courses.

That weekend, we agreed to see with our own eyes how the English courses were run. The course we attended was advanced, aimed at providing doctors with the English skills necessary to communicate with patients and colleagues. The students were also advanced, having already taken primer courses. I had studied some English at the Institute in Lithuania, a branch of the University of Latvia, so I was not a beginner. However, dropping right into that advanced course was not easy. I had to learn a lot of new medical terms in English, and how to use those terms when conversing with patients.

That said, the lessons were interesting and we were warmly accepted. We soon became more closely acquainted with our new colleagues, some of whom are still friends to this day. In the evenings, we had barbecues and karaoke parties where we spoke only in English. It was fun and very useful to speak in English in an informal setting.

We established links with an agency in the UK that specialised in finding work there for doctors. When my husband contacted the agency, they immediately began to search for a job for him, while preparing the necessary documents. As a nurse, I was not able to benefit from their assistance, so I turned my attention elsewhere, researching various agencies that dealt specifically with nurses.

I was very cautious, because I had read many sad stories in the press about people who had been defrauded by dishonest agencies. I later met people in England who had suffered in this way. They told me that some agencies advertised jobs, took money from their customers, transported them to England, and then disappeared, leaving the customers stranded. I realised that I could only rely upon serious organisations.

Searching through the newspaper advertisements, I found a firm in Vilnius that said it could help me find employment in England with Bupa, a well-known private healthcare company. I did my research on Bupa, and after reviewing the work offered – and learning that the agency would not charge me for their services – I decided to sign up.

I was invited to Vilnius for an interview, which would be conducted over the phone with a potential employer in England. I had never spoken English on the telephone before, and I was so nervous that all my knowledge of the language evaporated. Of course, I was not successful.

As I was so determined to leave Lithuania for England, I took a risk, signing up with an agency that charged for its services. Once I made the payment, I began to receive calls from potential employers in England who were interested in hearing about my nursing experience.

I concentrated, and this time, I was able to speak English much better, answering their various questions. The calls were long and we spoke a lot. Sometimes I got my words mixed up, but my confidence grew, and I spoke better as the conversations became longer. I look back today at those conversations and I smile: "Well, I was stubborn..."

Not long after, I received another call from the agency. They said that they had found a job for me and I should prepare to move to England soon. I was worried about what lay in store for me, but I calmed down a little when I learned that the job was near London. If it turned out to be a scam and I was left on the street, I would be able to contact some of my Lithuanian acquaintances living in London and stay with them for a while.

I hastily packed my suitcases. My husband did not try to dissuade me. We decided that if we waited until he was offered a job in England, it might be too late for me.

I told myself: "I'm going first; I'll have a look around, and then he will come later."

Foggy Albion

For those of you who do not know – or may have forgotten – I would like to describe a place called "Albion". There is no country of that name in the modern world; it cannot be found on modern maps. Rather, Albion is an ancient name for Britain, that island comprising the modern nations of England, Scotland and Wales.

Albion means "White Land", probably a reference to the spectacular White Cliffs of Dover, which visitors (or invaders) would have seen on arrival by boat. Some people, however, believe it refers to the foggy weather for which Britain is famous.

The name is thought to be Celtic in origin, derived from "albus", the Latin word for "white". It was first mentioned in ancient Greek sources during the fifth or sixth century BC. The Romans, who invaded England in AD 43, used the name Albion, although their own name for the place – "Britain" – later prevailed.

Albion to this day is used as a poetic name for England. It was widely prevalent in nineteenth century fiction and I must admit to liking it. It has an appealing, mysterious sound, suggestive of old castles, mist-shrouded valleys and allegedly supernatural phenomena. It was to this "Foggy Albion" that I was determined to go.

When I had first signed up with the agency in Lithuania, I fully expected that my work would be in London or one of its suburbs. However, as my day of departure came closer, I learned that the job was somewhere quite different – in the northern city of Leeds. Before boarding the plane to London, I spoke with a woman from the agency who gave me the address in Leeds. She said that the people there would organise my documents and direct me to my workplace.

I travelled to "my Albion" for the first time on the 23rd of August 2005, arriving alone at London's Stansted Airport. As I mingled with the people in the crowded airport and listened to them speaking, I felt like I'd been hit over the head.

"This is England?" I thought. "What language are they speaking? This is not the language that I learned!"

Such was my first impression of the various dialects around me; I seemed to be swamped in a sea of foreign-speaking people. Luckily, at the airport information office, I was able to communicate in English and understand what I was told.

Everything was new to me and there was a lot of excitement, but I realised that I had to concentrate and think about what to do, where to go and what I needed. The journey to my first place of work was going to be long and intricate, and I had to focus.

I bought a bus ticket and started on my journey to Leeds, which was not at all close. I travelled all night, and on arrival I took a taxi to the agency's office. At the agency, people were arriving from everywhere, and their objective was the same as mine: to get a job. I didn't meet anyone from Lithuania.

At the office, I learned that I would work as a nurse's assistant – also called a "care assistant". I would be paid the minimum hourly wage, which was £4.85 in England at that time. I was disappointed that I was not being offered work as a qualified nurse. In Lithuania I had worked as a medical sister, and I was convinced that I would immediately get similar work in England. I did not understand yet that the English health system was very different from the Lithuanian one; that I must overcome various obstacles to reach my goal.

I was told that I would be working in Southport, a city on the west coast of England, 17 miles north of Liverpool. I was very surprised that I was being sent to Southport because the agency had not mentioned the place at all.

I called the woman from the Lithuanian agency to find out what was happening. Why was I being offered poorly-paid care assistant work? She explained that I would have to go back to London, where another agent would meet me and explain everything. Before heading back down to London, however, I had to complete the employment documents at the office in Leeds. This took all day, so I was obliged to stay overnight at a hotel.

The next morning, I journeyed back down to London. While I was on the bus, I received a call from a man who spoke in English. I wasn't quite sure who he was, but he was unhappy that I was not taking the job in Southport. He offered to meet me at Euston railway station in London, where we would discuss my options. I did not understand anything that was going on – but I had to trust him.

We met at Euston as arranged, and it became clear that he was the manager of the agency in Lithuania. He said that I should take the job I was offered in Southport, and using my money, he bought me a train ticket for the next day. He said I could spend the night in an empty cottage on the outskirts of London, an area mostly inhabited by newcomers from Asia.

Just to make my situation more complicated, as I was preparing to return to Southport, I received a phone call from someone offering me a job in London. The man on the phone said the job was mine if I wanted it; all I had to do was get on a bus to the workplace. He was even willing to pay for my ticket across London. It was very tempting, but I declined the offer. After all, who was to know whether it would be better or worse than Southport?

My thoughts were racing by now. I knew the agent's communications to be poor, so I wasn't so surprised to find some confusion over where I would be working. But I faced another problem: where was London? Apparently, I was in London already, but I felt like I hadn't really seen it. My impressions of the city were based solely on Euston station and the area in which I stayed overnight.

Of course, I didn't have time to think too deeply about London and how it looked. I was thinking only about my own safety, and about tomorrow's trip to Southport, where my new job was waiting for me. Despite the confusion and various difficulties, I was accompanied everywhere by a silent feeling of joy; after all, I had not yet been cheated or left alone on the street.

Yes, there had been some confusion, but everything was working out just right. Looking back, I don't regret a single moment of those first few days. After all, I'm an optimist, and I believe in Fate. Wherever Fate leads you is where you're meant to be.

Like a kitten in water

In Southport, I was given accommodation shared by employees at the same place of work. The workers were of various nationalities, and I was very happy to discover that among them was a Lithuanian woman. I shared a room with an Icelandic woman who enjoyed chatting, and I was happy for the opportunity to practice my English.

The day after I moved into my lodgings, I was given directions to my new place of work. I went there to get acquainted with my workplace – a small, private nursing home for elderly people. The manager was cold, but she introduced me to a Lithuanian woman who worked there, instructing her to show me my duties.

These involved the daily care of the residents, including feeding, washing and dressing them, taking them to the bathroom, and monitoring their skin and health conditions. Any status changes had to be reported to the nurse. Care assistants were not required to carry the patients. For this purpose, there were special lifting devices called hoists or standing aids. I appreciated that what was being asked of me was a serious and responsible job.

There were three Lithuanians working in the nursing home: two women and a young man. We became friends and have stayed in contact since then. One of the Lithuanians, a woman named Jolanta, was a qualified nurse. She explained that the facility employed people as care assistants rather than nurses, regardless of their qualifications.

In order to work as a nurse, she said, I would have to apply to the Nursing and Midwifery Council (NMC) for a professional qualification number. Only then could I start applying for real nursing jobs in England. In Lithuania, I already had my nursing license, but to get my number in the UK, I would need to get various documents sent over from Vilnius.

The manager at the nursing home said that I would be summoned to work as soon as they had checked my criminal history. I had already provided the results of a criminal record check from Lithuania. However, the rules required that a further check be conducted using the UK's own criminal records database.

The situation was somewhat different for people who already had the appropriate professional registration in the UK – such as qualified nurses with the relevant number. In such cases, no questions were asked about a possible criminal record.

It took over a week for my UK criminal record check to be completed. As I waited, not knowing when I would begin work, I wondered how I would survive with no income. I felt like a kitten paddling about in a river, struggling to keep its head above water. There was no telling whether I would make a success of this move to a strange country.

The good news was that in England at that time – at least in the Southport area – one could do all one's grocery shopping on just £15 a week. In the Asda supermarket, where I usually shopped, it was possible to buy good food at a very low price. I wondered why Lithuania was not like this.

With a lot of free time on my hands, I walked around the town in order to get acquainted with the English way of living. Many things surprised me. For one thing, I saw many people walking around the streets in their work uniforms. There were people dressed as sales assistants and bar staff, for example, as well as nurses. In England, it seemed that no one changed from their uniforms into their normal clothes when they left work.

I was particularly puzzled by the doctors and nurses, wearing the same white uniforms on the streets as they had worn in clinical settings. To me, this did not look right. It was also contrary to the requirements of sanitation, which is an important factor when working with sick and injured people. After a while, I also became a part of that crowd, but I never let myself be seen outside of my working environment wearing my working clothes.

There was also inconsistency in dress codes, with many doctors working without their medical coats, wearing casual clothes instead. At the nursing home where I worked, it was often impossible to distinguish between a doctor and an everyday visitor.

England is a tolerant country, affording basic rights to its diverse and multi-ethnic workforce. However, some of the sights were a surprise to me, newly arrived from Lithuania. For example, I had never before seen doctors wearing headscarves and floor-sweeping skirts. Nor had I seen Indian doctors wearing turbans in their offices. It was good to know that they changed their clothes before entering the operating rooms. In England, as everywhere else in the world, the same rule applies: the theatre must be sterile.

In the following years, I would work in various retirement homes, nursing homes and hospitals, and I learned that infectious diseases – including MRSA and scabies – are fairly common. Indeed, it is still the case that patients often pick up infections at hospitals and other medical facilities in England.

My first workplace

At last, I was summoned to start work. It was only my first day on the job, but already I was confronted with a new shock. Many of the nursing home residents spoke in a regional dialect of English, and for this reason I was assigned to work with another Lithuanian.

I had to admit that I could not understand what the residents were saying. It was explained to me later that they were speaking with a Liverpool accent, which even the British have difficulty with. Added to which, of course, the English that I had learned in Lithuania was far from perfect.

However, I set to my work with enthusiasm, and in the following weeks I began to get the hang of things. Due to the constant need for communication with the residents, and also with my colleagues, my knowledge of English improved rapidly. In the process, I learned a great deal about English cuisine and eating habits, as well as the daily routines, way of life and the traditions of the people. I gave myself an added boost by signing up for college and attending English-language courses.

I also had to attend college courses in nursing practice. These covered health-and-safety issues, such as patient safety and the correct methods for lifting patients. Despite the emphasis on the safety of care assistants, there were still occasional incidents at work, including back injuries. We were instructed in the use of special lifting equipment to try to reduce such incidents. We were also shown various nursing measures that required specialist knowledge. Overall, I was impressed with the range of measures to facilitate the work of nursing staff and ensure patient safety in England.

One thing I was not impressed with, however, was the rule that care assistants working in nursing homes must operate in pairs, even when not required to physically move a patient. The rule is based on the principle that there should always be a third person in any care situation who can provide evidence in case of claims of wrongdoing. This rule is designed to protect patients from mistreatment, but also to protect staff from unfair allegations.

In my job, this rule became a problem whenever we had a shortage of staff. It would have been helpful if the care assistants were allowed to perform certain tasks alone, but this was not permitted, and it often slowed us down. Such rules did not apply in Lithuania, and I found myself getting quite upset at the situation I now found myself in. In Lithuania I had worked in a clinic and later in a sanatorium. There I took the attitude that all jobs, no matter how menial, had to be done – with or without additional help.

It is commonly said that the work of a care assistant can be exhausting, low-paid and not fully appreciated. This first job in England fitted this description well. There was a lot to be done each day, including physical tasks such as washing, dressing and feeding the residents. I will describe these tasks in more detail later in the book. For now, let me just say how glad I was to have started work in England at last. My English dream was finally becoming a reality, for which I was truly grateful.

A second attempt

I worked for just three months in England before return-
ing to Lithuania in the autumn of 2005. My husband was
still waiting for a job offer in England, and I wanted to be
with him.

I was only in Vilnius for a few days before I received a
phone call from an agency. It was the same agency that
had supplied me with my first – and disastrous – telephone interview. They wondered whether my English
had improved, and if I was still looking for work.

After all my practice in Southport, I easily impressed
them with my English over the phone. They invited me
to a meeting in Vilnius with a prospective employer:
Bupa. The interview with the Bupa representative went
so well that, as I sat there in the office, I already knew
that I would get the job.

I was pleased with the outcome, but this time I didn't want
to go to England by myself. I told the representative that
my husband was looking for work as a doctor in England,
and I wanted to wait for him to sign a contract before I
relocated again. I said I was hoping to get a job in the
same general location as my husband. The company
agreed to my conditions. Now it was just a matter of waiting.

In 2006, my husband finally signed a contract for a job in
Staffordshire, in the English West Midlands. To fit with
his plans, Bupa offered me a one-year contract at one of
their nursing homes in Walsall, not far from my

husband's new job. It was all working out as planned, and very soon we were ready for departure.

Lithuanians moving to England to work for Bupa were normally met at the airport in London by a company representative. In this way, new arrivals were not required to wander about looking for transportation and accommodation; rather, they were taken directly to the right place and provided with somewhere to stay.

My husband and I were a little different, because we arrived in England by car, not by plane. However, Bupa was still very good at looking after us. We were settled into a hotel, all expenses paid, including food. Soon after that, a two-bedroom house was found for us. The deposit and half the rent were paid by the company. My husband and I were both getting free meals at work, so that helped reduce costs too.

I was very pleased by Bupa's sense of responsibility toward its employees. I still have work assignments at a Bupa nursing home sometimes, and so far as I know, they still treat their employees in this responsible manner.

I soon started work at the nursing home, where I was employed as a nursing assistant – basically the same role as I was performing in Southport. Once again, I found that communicating with the residents was a challenge at times, partly because my English still wasn't great. However, through my interactions with both staff and patients, I began to get more insight into British English – including some culturally specific expressions.

I met one resident, a very intelligent elderly man who had worked as a teacher, and we soon became friends. He taught me English pronunciation and awareness of various dialects. He also told me a variety of funny stories, enabling me to better understand English humour. In this way, he said, I would not be insulted by hearing ambiguous English expressions. To the uninitiated foreigner, such expressions can sometimes sound quite different from the intended meaning.

For example, English people like to address their friends, companions, acquaintances or even clients with sweet and nice-sounding words. However, at first, such expressions did not always seem appropriate to me. In English culture, it is common to address some as "love". In Lithuanian, calling someone "love" when you don't know them well would be considered an insult.

When I was first addressed in this way – by a Pakistani nurse – I was confused and angry.

"What kind of person am I to you?" I demanded.

I later realised that it was just a friendly English greeting – no more and no less.

I subsequently came to learn many different ways to greet people, some of them specific to particular regions of England, such as: "chick", "duck" "cock" and "mate". All of these words are just friendly ways of addressing another person, and I was glad to have learned this crucial information.

The same topic was raised during a short nursing course that I was sent on when I started at the nursing home. Part of the course was about communicating with both patients and colleagues. We had to show respect and empathy, addressing patients with affectionate terms such as "love", "sweetheart", "dear" and "darling". In England, such terms are used everywhere – by shop cashiers, restaurant waiting staff, hospital nurses, and even the passers-by in the street, regardless of age.

I started taking English courses at a local college. I was studying alongside other English people, in a small group of just five students, all of whom were having problems with their own language. I was surprised to find that one of the students – a British person – was completely illiterate.

This man was a farmer and an otherwise very capable and practical individual, in full-time employment. He studied individual letters of the alphabet to help him read. I found his problem with reading and writing to be quite unusual. It wasn't due to dyslexia, but rather from lack of education.

Another man was studying English in order to gain a higher position at work. He needed to pass the English exam and obtain a certificate at an appropriate level. The group also included two mentally disabled people.

Another peculiarity of the English language is the way that measures of time are used, which is quite different from the Lithuania approach. The English like to say, "Just a minute" or "It will only take a minute". Or else they say, "I will be there in a minute" or "I will do it in a minute." However, as I soon discovered, when an English person says they will be with you in a minute, they don't mean literally one minute. They mean they'll be there as soon as they can. Compared with Lithuanians, the British are usually not so prompt.

I also took some time to get my head around the different ways the word "problem" is also used – depending on whether there is a problem or there isn't. For example, sometimes it's used in response to expressions of gratitude. If someone says, "Thank you," the response is often, "No problem". This can mean that there really were no problems, or perhaps that there were some problems – but the person has no problem with the problems!

The work "alright" took a bit of getting used to as well. In one context, it means that everything is okay, but in another context it just means, "Good morning!"

I soon discovered that people of different nationalities behave quite differently in similar situations. The British, I found out, use many words to express gratitude and apology, which is not something Lithuanians would do. If you step on a British person's foot, they are more likely to say sorry than swear at you!

Of course, this does not necessarily mean that they want to be on friendly terms with you. They may even be uttering obscenities under their breath.

Learning how to apply a foreign language in conjunction with a nation's character, its customs and philosophy, can be problematical. But with a bit of effort and some help

from those around me, I was slowly getting the hang of
it.

The care assistant's job

The job of a care assistant in a nursing home is not easy, involving both psychological and physical pressures. There is a lot to get done in the course of a working day, and one must always be attentive to the needs of the residents, regardless of the workload. Perhaps the best way of illustrating the challenges of the job is to show a typical care assistant's working day from start to end.

A full-time care assistant often works shifts of 12 hours or more, from 8am to 8pm or even 7am to 9pm. The key tasks for the day are assigned by a nurse or administrator of some kind, with one or more care assistants responsible for preparing breakfast, while others will dress the residents, and others give them a morning wash.

Breakfast is served to the residents according to their needs and wishes. Some residents will have their meals in their rooms, while others eat in the common areas. Some will be able to feed themselves and merely need the food delivered, while others will need help with the actual process of eating. In order to meet this array of needs, the kitchen staff and care assistants will divide the tasks, with some delivering food while others hand-feed the residents.

As with lunch and dinner, the residents are normally able to choose their preferred breakfast foods from a menu, with orders placed the previous day.

Washing and dressing is another crucial part of the morning routine. After the residents have been given a wash, they will be helped to dress, although some are quite able to do this for themselves. While care assistants often make suggestions on what to wear, the final decision rests with the resident, based on their own preferences. No matter how they want to dress, we will help them, providing as much or as little assistance as needed.

Once everyone has been dressed and fed, the staff will typically take a break of about 15 or 20 minutes. Then they will prepare the next important stage, which is a tea break for the residents at around 11am. This is a well-established British tradition and one that residents value highly. To quote the famous British prime minister William Gladstone: "Thank God for tea! What would the world be without tea! I am glad to be born after the discovery of tea."

As I learned early on, British people normally take milk in their tea; it's a rare person indeed who likes it black. The British usually cannot drink their tea without a biscuit of some sort, and so these are normally provided as a matter of course.

Tea breaks are also very important from a health point of view because elderly residents must get a certain quantity of liquids each day. Care assistants have to keep written records of the liquids that each resident consumes, including what was drunk, how much and when. This information is part of the patient's care plan, aimed at ensuring their wellbeing.

Next on the care assistant's list is lunch, followed by an afternoon tea break, and then at about 5pm comes dinner. Many British people refer to dinner as "tea time", while in Lithuania we called it "before dinner time". Once again, the residents are normally able to order their preferred dishes from a menu, and the same care is taken to ensure everyone gets properly fed. Some people only want a light dinner – such as crisps and sandwiches – although there are normally hot meals on the menu too.

Between 7pm and 8pm is "evening drinks" time. A range of hot beverages is usually served, including tea, hot chocolate, cocoa and Horlicks. If residents want a small snack later in the evening, this can also be arranged.

Once the final food and drinks have been served, it's time for some peace and quiet. Some residents will go to sleep, while others stay awake, enjoying a longer evening. Some prefer to watch television, while others read a book or chat with friends.

And so another day passes: get up, get dressed, eat, drink, spend the day, go to sleep.

Throughout the day, of course, residents also need to go to the toilet. It's part of the care assistant's job to help residents if they need help in the bathroom, including changing the incontinence underwear of those residents who use them.

Generally speaking, the amount of work that a care assistant puts in depends on the level of care that the residents require, with three categories identified in the UK. The first group includes residents who require minimal assistance or none at all. The second group consists of residents who are bedridden or unable to move their limbs. The third group includes people with mental disabilities:

those suffering from dementia, Alzheimer's, or who have other serious psychological problems.

Of course, the schedule outlined above describes the work of care assistants during the day. For those working at night, things are slightly different. At night, every two hours, the assistant must visit the residents' rooms, verify that they are okay, and change their underwear if necessary. Among the other nocturnal duties are resident surveys and cleaning tasks.

In order to carry out the work of a care assistant properly, endless patience is required. If there is a lack of patience at first, it often develops over time. And this is just one way in which a person can be changed for the better in the course of doing the job. By helping an elderly person, many care assistants become more intelligent, tolerant and patient, adapting to the needs of others, and learning how to satisfy those needs.

A clash with management

When I was working in Lithuania, I was told that working in nursing homes in Lithuania and England was as different as day and night. I was told that in England the work was easier, with more work tools and with a different approach to the patients.

It's true that employment conditions in England are different from those in Lithuania. However, after working for some time in England, I feel that the focus of the care system is the same – and it's the same around the world. Everywhere the goal is to care for the sick, the disabled, the frail and the elderly – to provide care for those who need it, whether through sickness or age.

Within England, I have found that the quality and attitude of managers varies from one nursing home or hospital to another. Everyone takes a different approach, whether it's a poor attitude or a nice one. Managing a nursing or medical environment is very difficult and stressful work, of course, but some managers make things worse by failing to care properly for their staff. For teamwork to be successful there needs to be a feeling of mutual respect.

While working in the Bupa nursing home, I had a clash with management that was caused – in my view – by my manager's negative attitude, and possibly her discrimination against foreigners. The disagreement centred around whether or not I should be allowed to work in a pair with another Lithuanian member of staff named Audrone. Like me, Audrone was a qualified nurse, but she was starting out in England as a nursing assistant, and we soon became friends. I have already mentioned that we were required to work in pairs, but when Audrone and I were on the same shift, we were always separated. Instead, we were paired with nurses of other nationalities.

We were told that we could never work together since we were from the same country and shared a native language other than English. For English employees, there was no such rule in force; the English staff were allowed to work together. Understandably, Audrone and I were upset, as we would have made a very good team.

It seems the decision was made to ensure that we didn't speak Lithuanian in front of the patients, which is quite understandable. However, the rule of only speaking English had already been made clear to us, and we were unlikely to break it. Indeed, from the very start, whenever we had spoken Lithuanian at work, we were told, "Speak English!"

I felt sure the problem could be solved more respectfully and did not require keeping us apart. I began to wonder if there was some other factor at play here. Was it perhaps discrimination against us as foreigners?

We began to feel some psychological pressure from some of the English staff members. We had done nothing wrong, but we were followed and kept under close observation. People were always watching how we conducted ourselves, and what we said to the nursing home residents. We were warned that we could not talk to each other in Lithuanian – even when we were not dealing with patients.

Our Indian nurse colleagues advised us that the rules being applied to Audrone and me were not correct. They told us not to tolerate such discrimination and to complain to the Bupa management. I agreed that what was happening was very wrong, and I had always known how to defend myself.

However, on this occasion I decided not to go running to the local Bupa office with my grievance. Instead, I called the nursing home manager who was responsible for making this strange rule. I knew English well enough to speak with her, and I demanded an explanation, asking why she felt it was necessary to spy on me. She apologised and our discussion did not descend into an argument – but our relationship became cold.

Subsequently, she kept her distance from me and made no attempt to engage me in conversation. If she needed anything from me, she would ask through other employees.

Audrone and I began to openly challenge the rule that nurses of the same national background could not work together, and suddenly everything turned upside down. They allowed us to work together, and all the hostility and discrimination ended.

Later on, an inspector from Bupa's head office visited, inviting me and Audrone for an interview together. She asked us if we had been treated well, if anyone had discriminated against us and if we were content in our work. Interestingly, she said nothing that led me to think that she was aware of our negative experiences. I said nothing to explain the unpleasant situation that Audrone and I had

been through, and so the matter was never officially recorded. We were just happy to get on with our jobs without
any unnecessary stress or bother.

Closer to my goal

Through working at Bupa, I finally got my papers in order and gained a PIN number from the NMC. In other words, I obtained my license to work as a nurse in the UK. Now I was keen to get a nurse's job, and I felt my prospects were good. I had always tried to do everything correctly in my job. I had also made friends with both the nurses and patients. After all, the nursing assistant is the closest person to the patient, spending more time with them than anyone else.

Unfortunately, Bupa didn't offer me work as a nurse. After the situation with Audrone and the nursing home manager, I don't think they trusted me. So, towards the end of my one-year contract in February 2007, I started to look elsewhere for work as a nurse. I found an agency in Birmingham that promised to help me take this important step. However, at that time, they could only get me work as a care assistant. English employers favour nurses who already have nursing experience in England – and this was one thing I lacked.

I decided to accept the care assistant work that the agency offered me. However, I had not yet finished my one-year contract with Bupa, which meant I was doing both jobs at the same time for a while. I was in over my head and I found it a difficult balancing act.

The agency sent me to work in various nursing homes, residential homes and hospitals, and I found myself working hard. The pressure was made worse by the fact that we often lacked sufficient personnel. However, I obtained some valuable experience in a wide range of settings, becoming better acquainted with both the work and with the nurses.

The harder you work, the better you understand not only your job, but also your potential, gaining increased confidence in your ability. I worked as a nursing auxiliary at both Birmingham and Walsall hospitals, and I soon realised that I was capable of succeeding at the next level. With this in mind, I sought the support of nursing colleagues in obtaining work as a qualified nurse.

I should perhaps say something about the daily routine in an English hospital. It starts the same way for both nurses and auxiliaries – with patient hygiene. The patients are washed and prepared for the day ahead, including getting dressed or into new nightclothes.

Later, the nurses hand out the medicines, while the auxiliaries take the patients' blood pressure, temperature and pulse. During all this, the staff talk to the patients, raising their mood. A kind word and a smile are as good as most medicines.

The nurses have a lot to organise, including patient consultations, doctors' visits, and various clinical procedures. Both nurses and care assistants are very busy and run around like hamsters on a wheel.

The British nursing system is quite complex, with various nursing grades and levels of independence, including chief nurses in hospitals, nurse practitioners working in GP clinics, and district nurses. Within hospitals, many nurses choose to specialise, developing and deepening particular skills as their careers progress.

When I first started working in British hospitals, I also came to learn of specialist jobs that I'd not encountered before, such as the phlebotomists, who take blood tests. To qualify as a phlebotomist, you don't need to be a nurse; you just take several short courses and obtain a certificate. Then you can work in hospitals, GP clinics and blood transfusion stations. Some specialise in blood testing, while others give IV treatment to patients.

Good phlebotomy professionals are valued because their work is very responsible and difficult. There is a lot of skill involved in puncturing a vein correctly, as well as inserting cannulas. Due to this skill level, phlebotomists earn more than nursing assistants, although not as much as qualified nurses.

In one hospital I remember being very surprised to read a message about the postponement of the insertion of a patient's IV drip because the phlebotomist was sick. The demand for phlebotomists in the UK is as high as for other nursing staff. However, recruitment of new phlebotomists requires proof of experience, and it is better if the experience is gained in the UK.

It was while working through the Birmingham agency that I began to understand the reasons why foreign workers were often distrusted. Most of them had come from Eastern European countries and they did not understand the British care system. These workers did not know the legal requirements of that system which could lead to complications and misunderstandings at times. Many of them were also unaware of their employment rights.

There had been articles in the Lithuanian press claiming that private nursing companies used Lithuanians as cheap labour. It's true that many Lithuanian care assistants were working for the minimum wage in the UK. However, this was true for people of all nationalities without exception, including people from India and the British staff.

I worked with people of many different nationalities during that period, some of whom were unfriendly or difficult, including several English and Filipino care assistants. It was the friendly women from India who always helped me and gave me advice. However, the nurses were all good-natured, and I made many long-term friends during that period.

A nurse at last

I continued to seek that all-important first nursing job, and my persistence led me to a Wolverhampton nursing agency that was recruiting nursing staff of various sorts. I was invited to an interview with the agency's director, and after greetings and polite exchanges, we began a serious conversation about the profession.

My approach was based on my previous experiences, and I was determined to let her know that I had been discriminated against and denied the trust that I deserved. I said I was having a hard time getting accepted as a nurse in England, and had been set to work only with other foreign nurses.

I asked: "What's the difference between me, a Pakistani or a Filipino nurse?"

I told her everything – that even though I was *upset* at that time, this should not detract from my ability to work as a nurse. But under no circumstances would I accept another care assistant job.

After politely listening to me, the agency director calmly told me to ask questions that were not concerned with negatives, but related to the duties of a nurse.

I was ashamed and sorry for my unprofessional behaviour during my introduction. The rest of our conversation went very well, and I was over the moon when I was offered work as a qualified nurse in a nursing home.

I could not believe it when she said how much I would be paid by the hour. Since I did not understand the numbers completely, I thought that maybe I had heard incorrectly. In May 2007, I became a licensed nurse working in England.

Working through an agency suited me well, and I enjoyed the variety and flexibility it offered. Agency workers may be called upon to work at numerous care homes and hospitals, often moving quickly from one place to another. Key employees are called upon to fill gaps due to illness, annual leave or general staffing shortages. When managers find they are short of staff, they call the agencies and arrange for nurses or nursing assistants to be sent out. Agency staff are paid by the hour, and they may be called on to do many hours one week and very few the next.

However, they can also stipulate what sorts of work they are willing to do and what hours suit them best. During the nine years I worked in nursing homes, I was mostly able to pick those locations with a pleasant atmosphere and good staff. That does not mean this period of my life was uneventful; just about everything that could happen did happen. The work was not easy and there was a lot of responsibility on my shoulders. I was always being told to do everything by the book and document every step carefully. The words "Cover yourself" were always in the air.

I also worked as a 'bank nurse' during this period, which means working directly for the employer, but as a temporary worker with flexible hours. Nursing banks were set up to provide staff to fill staffing gaps, providing an alternative to the traditional nursing agency model. This was really good for me, because I was able to choose when I worked, with my schedule written out one week at a time. If I needed a night off, I just said that I couldn't work on that night. I also found it easier to travel to Lithuania or elsewhere on vacation.

The agencies also provided me with my first jobs caring for people in their own homes. These patients included the terminally ill, those with chronic debilitating conditions and the elderly.

The Wolverhampton agency that first hired me as a nurse subsequently closed down, but their staff went to other agencies, taking me with them. To this day, I am still working with my first director, although I am now working with my third agency. Employment agency staff change and move on; they gain experience and connections and then open their own agencies. Very often they will stay in touch with nurses with whom they've built productive relationships. And so the circle turns.

I am now loyal to the Kare Plus agency, having worked for them since 2010. I like the team and the relationships we have. However, much has changed since I was first offered a nursing job. At first, I was employed through the agency, but now I work as a subcontractor. In other words, I have my own personal business, and the agency hires me under contract. In the UK, many people work in this way.

I'm happy to say that, as I was advancing my nursing career in England, my husband was doing the same with his career as a doctor. When I was working with Bupa, he was working for the Staffordshire Ambulance Service on a six-month contract. In England, ambulance services of this kind employ professional paramedics, specially trained to respond to the scene of medical emergencies. However, in Staffordshire the ambulance service was also employing doctors as part of their clinical team, going out to treat patients wherever required. My husband's station was the first and only ambulance station in England to make use of doctors in this way. There were three doctors employed there, all of them Lithuanians.

The programme for which my husband worked delivered both scheduled and unscheduled services across the West Midlands. He was greeted by the patients with gratitude and joy, receiving many thank-you letters from them. His work at Staffordshire was recognised for its excellence and professionalism, and he was awarded certificates. I am very proud of him.

However, before his six months in Staffordshire were up, the agency from Lithuania that had promised to find him work invited him for an interview. He was successful, securing a new job as a disability assessor. The ambulance station asked him to stay on for another three-month period, and he agreed to do so, working both jobs simultaneously for a while, just as I had done previously. Finally, however, he waved goodbye to the ambulance service and settled into his new job. Today, he continues to follow his passion for medicine, working as an occupational health physician.

The nursing merry-go-round

Sometimes, working as a nurse feels like being on a merry-go-round: you are always moving, never still for a moment. Actually, the daily routine can be quite demanding, with plenty of stress to keep the body and mind active.

Working hours vary greatly, but in a nursing home – where I've spent most of my time – the day shift is often from 8am to 8pm. Personally, I am more likely to start at 7:15am and finish around 9pm, so that's a very long day!

A typical working day begins with a short meeting or report, which we Lithuanians call a "five-minute". The nurses review each and every resident, including how they have been feeling and the details of the services/procedures provided.

We then look at our logs and diaries to see what each resident needs in the coming day in terms of actions and procedures. This includes taking blood for blood tests that have been prescribed by the doctors. It might also involve ordering medications, inviting a GP to see a resident, ordering a car for a resident to be referred to a specialist's consultation, or any number of other procedures or services. We nurses will be doing much of this while the care assistants are looking after the residents' more basic needs, such as washing, dressing and eating breakfast.

Medications are generally dispersed from 8am to 11.30am, although sometimes we might overrun by half an hour or so. If a care assistant notices the slightest change on a patient's body – such as a wound or bruise –

they are required to tell the nurses. It is then up to the nurse to approach the patient, assess the situation and make decisions.

For example, if the problem is a sore, the nurse must decide if it is necessary to give treatment. Any treatment should be recorded in the nursing plan, while a photograph is taken, the problem reported to the administrator, the information faxed to the family doctor, and the relatives informed.

After completing the distribution of medicines, we nurses follow our diary, doing everything that is specified there. This includes everything relating to appointments, transfers, hospital visits, social workers, physiotherapists and doctors. After that, we might have a 20-minute break – if there's time.

At 1pm we serve lunch and hand out more medicines. Around 1:30pm or 2pm there is another meeting, because around 2pm many of the employees are changing shifts. The nurse in charge provides information about the situation in her department and the entire team adjusts accordingly.

I really like teamwork. When I need to know something, I only have to ask, and I get an answer straight away. The care assistants know almost everything.

We have 30 minutes for lunch, and at night we get a rest break of one hour. After the lunch break, we write care plans containing many details and observations. During the course of the shift, I communicate with a wide range of colleagues, including physiotherapists, doctors, social workers, and other professionals who come to work with our residents. All of their observations are also recorded in the nurse's care plans and daily records.

Before 5pm I start checking the blood of the diabetics. After which, it is time to administer insulin and other medicines during the "evening circle" routine. Some patients are fed through a feeding machine (PEG), and it is necessary to closely monitor the progress of this process to ensure a sufficient supply of liquids.

There are many different things we do that are not related to clinical treatment, but without which our relationships with the residents would be unimaginable. For example, sometimes a nurse becomes a beauty salon employee – combing the residents' hair or putting cream on their faces. Sometimes you are simply a close friend – giving them a kiss at bedtime and wishing them sweet dreams.

We do not write such activities into our logs, but it's our duty as caring human beings. It could not be otherwise. You just feel responsible for that person and for the duty that you as a nurse should perform.

There is quite a different system for working the night shift, which I sometimes do. The duties of a night nurse include the provision and reviewing of the existing stocks of medicines, as well as writing nursing plans. We also monitor various factors in the health of the residents, including nutrition, liquids and mucous membranes.

Mostly, though, I am on the day shift, where things are always in motion: it never stops. Nurses must take all their energy and share it with their colleagues and patients – and then find some more to share.

And just where does the strength come from? It should be said that nurses in the UK are not left without help. Seminars, training sessions and refresher courses are frequently provided, both through their employers and through umbrella organisations such as the Nursing and Midwifery Council. Nurses are taught new skills relating to patient care, management and broader skills, such as stress management. It's encouraging to know that, in Britain, the work of nurses is valued and their training is taken seriously.

The variety of life

My work as an agency nurse has provided me with a great deal of variety, both in terms of working environments and the types of patients I've worked with. I have worked in residential care homes, nursing homes, private residences and homes for those suffering severe disabilities. While most of my patients have been elderly, there have also been quite a few middle-aged and younger people, including those who have suffered serious accidents. Some have been long-term residents with whom I've had the opportunity to build deeper relationships. Others have been passing through, in need of a period of recovery before moving on elsewhere. Meanwhile, many of those I've cared for have passed away, leaving behind grieving relatives – as well as being missed by the nurses and other staff.

Among the most rewarding patients to work with are those who arrive at a nursing home in poor shape and leave it looking and feeling much better. Sometimes they come from hospital for a period of rehabilitation following a downturn in their health or some traumatic incident such as a fractured hip. They stay for six weeks before moving somewhere else, whether that be another nursing home, a residential care home or sheltered accommodation.

The term "rehabilitation" has different implications in different countries. In Lithuania, for example, rehabilitation often occurs in a sanatorium, which seems more like a hotel equipped with various spa treatments. There are massage and kinesiotherapy (physiotherapy) treatments, often making use of the swimming pool. Patients perform exercises in water, take mineral and mud baths, relax in the jacuzzi and enjoy underwater massage. There are holistic therapies, such as aromatherapy and audiotherapy. Meanwhile, psychotherapy is available for those who need it. The curative mud and mineral-water treatments depend on the deposits owned by the health resorts.

The range of spa services available in the Lithuanian system seeks to restore the patient's physical strength and bring back the joy of life.

While such a range of services is not normally available in the UK system, there are many effective rehabilitation services provided. For example, the physiotherapists in nursing homes help the patients greatly. I really admire the work they do, performing little miracles in facilitating the recovery of people who seemed hopeless. People come with mobility issues that prevent them from doing everyday tasks such as getting out of bed. But after six weeks, they often find the problem is solved, and they are able to walk about unaided. Finally, they go home with little help!

I have also worked with people suffering from serious disabilities, often the result of traumatic injuries such as traffic accidents. The institutions where these people reside are also called nursing homes, but the patients are often quite young. Our job as nurses and care assistants was to make these unfortunate people more comfortable and to bring them a better quality of life.

While rehabilitation does not always allow such people to walk out of the nursing home, we are able to brighten their lives in various ways. And for those who would be ending their lives in such a nursing home, it is our job to ensure their final days and hours are as easy and comfortable as possible. This focus on quality of life is one of the things I like most about the UK's healthcare system.

I have also worked with people suffering from a range of chronic and debilitating diseases, which can affect both body and mind. Again, in addition to the purely clinical care, one of our chief responsibilities was to ensure an improved quality of life, wherever possible. Very often, a patient's day can be brightened simply by engaging in an interesting conversation with those around them. Like many care assistants and nursing staff, I have enjoyed many interesting conversations with patients like these. They have shared their views and life stories, also teaching me about British life and habits. In this way, the patients have also helped to enrich my own life.

Working with such people brought me some valuable life lessons too, including the importance of a positive – or at least accepting – attitude to life. I admired the fact that almost everybody was happy with the hand that Fate had dealt them. They gladly spoke about the achievements of their lives, no matter how small. In many cases, it was obvious that their lives had not been so great, but their complaints were far and few between.

Among the most debilitating conditions to strike people in later life are Alzheimer's and senile dementia. These conditions, which impair both memory and cognition, are very common throughout the world, and the UK is no exception. Aside from daily nursing care, such patients often need help with remembering things and remaining oriented, as well as dealing with the anxiety and panic that such conditions sometimes cause.

When I first started to work with patients suffering from Alzheimer's and dementia, I found myself suffering from huge emotional stress. It was not only the pressure of the work itself, but also the troubling thoughts that such an environment can provoke. I began to wonder at the point of life if it must end with such a hopelessly painful disease.

I witnessed their suffering up close and became very sensitive to their situation, filled with sorrow for these people who had lost their self-esteem.

As I got to know these patients, I learned more about their lives, and all that they had experienced and accomplished. I saw the photos from their youth, filled with life, loving, caring and happiness. And now I could see them after disease had taken its toll, changing them forever. It caused a terrible pain in my heart and a feeling of hopelessness in my soul.

I began to realise that if it were not for the concern and compassion we nurses were able to provide, the emptiness in their lives might never be filled.

Nursing as a vocation

The profession of nursing wouldn't be what it is today if nurses felt they were doing a job like any other. In order to keep going back, day after day, year after year, they must feel the value of the service they provide to those in need. They must be committed to nursing as a vocation, a career choice based on compassionate motivations and with a proud history.

While working in England, I soon came to learn about Florence Nightingale, the English woman widely viewed as the founder of the modern nursing profession. She organised the treatment of wounded soldiers during the Crimean War in the 1850s, setting standards for nursing care that were the basis for the nursing profession. She and her team of nurses saved countless lives during the war, emphasising the importance of cleanliness and proper care for the sick and injured.

Thanks to an 1855 article in *The Times* newspaper, Nightingale gained the nickname "The Lady with the Lamp" for her tireless work during the Crimean War:

"She is a 'ministering angel' without any exaggeration in these hospitals, and as her slender form glides quietly along each corridor, every poor fellow's face softens with gratitude at the sight of her. When all the medical officers have retired for the night and silence and darkness have settled down upon those miles of prostrate sick, she may be observed alone, with a little lamp in her hand, making her solitary rounds."

She also went on to establish a school of nursing at St Thomas' Hospital in London, the world's first secular nursing school. The school has now been moved to Kings' College, but it continues to provide high-quality nursing education. It inspired the spread of nursing schools around the world, many of which now provide bachelor's degrees and postgraduate qualifications in nursing studies.

Like many nurses, I find the story of Florence Nightingale inspiring, and her dedication and sense of vocation is just as relevant today as it ever was. Working in nursing homes, nurses and care assistants are exposed to a great deal of mental and emotional pressure. After all, the residents are nearing the end of their lives, which means they face both physical difficulties and the fears and regrets often associated with death.

It is often emotionally hard to look after people who are receiving end-of-life care, but we focus on carrying out the care plans for each resident, while offering them a caring and gentle attitude. While there are frequent difficulties, we can also see how our efforts are helping and it's gratifying when residents express their appreciation – as they often do.

After years as a nurse in nursing homes, I still love my work. I often feel more at home in my workplace than I do at home. I am so proud to be a member of this fine, caring profession, and I am confident that I know my job well, making me able to cope with just about any situation that arises.

I work long hours, sometimes 12 or 14 hours per day, and although I get tired, I am happy at the end of a shift that I have left the residents calm and happy. Since I spend so much time with the residents, I get to know their needs and personalities, and I often feel that I've become like a part of their extended family. I listen to their stories, as well as their aches and complaints, and I'm always mindful of my mission of helping those in need.

Many people learn of the work of doctors and nurses from watching TV shows and films. From such dramas, it's clear how busy they are during the course of a working day. But what TV shows and movies can't communicate is the depth of feeling one has for a resident or patient suffering from a serious condition such as dementia or Alzheimer's. Nor indeed for those facing imminent death or breathing their last breaths. Nothing can communicate the depth of feeling that such situations evoke.

Of course, we have work to do, so we have to keep our feelings in check to some degree. In particular, we have to control our frustrations when we're called upon to comfort someone at 3am, when we'd rather be fast asleep ourselves. It's often in the early hours that a resident will have a bad dream and ask us to phone their son or daughter, or perhaps just offer some comfort and fluff up their pillows. And then there are those very trying moments when relatives get angry at you for something out of your control, perhaps shouting at you because you don't know when the consultant will be visiting.

Yes, this job would be all the more draining if we didn't view it as a vocation; a career that adds meaning to our lives. The days are long, and by the end, I just want to go home and relax in silence, without talking to anyone. The next morning comes, and I prepare for work, calmly and happily anticipating another day – and I realise that I love my life and wouldn't want to change a thing.

Bad habits

There has been much debate about what factors shorten a human lifespan. Among the conclusions is that the chief culprit is life-shortening bad habits. Yes, harmful habits are of great importance, and I have worked with many senior citizens who have suffered the consequences of irresponsible lifestyle choices.

One female patient once asked me if I smoked.

- "No, I don't," I said. "I don't need it."
- "Well, don't ever start smoking," she said. "See how painfully I pay for my weakness, how much I suffer for this bad habit."

This woman could clearly see the error of her ways. But there are many others who continue to smoke right up to the end of their lives, despite the harm this causes them. And we nurses are not permitted to stop them. Nursing homes even have smoking areas, and we must push them there in their wheelchairs to indulge their habit.

Another harmful lifestyle is alcoholism. It is a habit that many people indulge even after they move into a nursing home. I often find bottles of alcohol in the residents' rooms that have been brought there by relatives. Such things are not against the rules.

Some residents are given alcoholic drinks every evening. I remember the first time I saw this, and I found it hard to believe. It was an elderly woman who had whisky in hot water every evening during the evening tea break. When I saw this drink – known as a "hot toddy" – I was surprised, because I'd never come across it before. But I soon discovered that it's quite popular with older people in Britain.

Another woman had a glass of ginger wine each evening, and I would have to deliver it to her. Each time I brought the lady her wine, she gave me a lecture on how healthy the ginger was for her joints. She was suffering from arthritis and was unable to walk.

These two drinks are often seen as "winter warmers", and old ladies in particular enjoy their ginger wine.

Another patient would scream if we did not give her as much alcohol as she wanted. We had no time to argue with her, because we had to take care of the rest of the residents.

Generally speaking, we follow the philosophy that a person can use for their own pleasure anything they wish – and as much of it as they want. We nurses have to accept each person for what they are, warts and all.

Some residents are calm, thoughtful and well meaning, with good habits. Helping such people is relatively easy. However, there are many others whose bad habits or bad attitude can be trying, and that's when we have to make a special effort.

Some people have been spoiled throughout their lives, acting selfishly and always demanding more for themselves, regardless of the impact on others. Dealing with such people, we nurses must endure lots of whining and complaining. Sometimes our patience is drawn very thin, but then we stop, take an inspirational breath, count up to 10 – as psychologists teach us on courses – and try to gently continue performing our duties.

Other patients are difficult due to the nature of their condition. They may have an illness that affects their personality, causing confusion or anger, and in such cases, they cannot be blamed for their bad actions. In such situations, a nurse can only be patient and offer to help.

This is the responsibility of the nurses – to provide assistance in old age without judging the patient or wondering how much they deserve from life. Everyone has the right to good nursing care in old age.

The desire to live

One evening I had to speak with one of the residents of the nursing home where I worked. He was over 80 years old and his words were strained. Every one of his words spoke of weakness and despair; it was as if he was no longer among the living. He complained that his life no longer made sense and that he was no longer needed.

- "We are born, we grow up, we raise children; then we get older, we become a burden to ourselves, and finally a burden to others – and this is the end," he said.

I realised that the man had abandoned his desire to live because he felt useless to everyone. As long as he had felt needed, he was able to enjoy nature, the sun and the blue sky, remembering the most beautiful moments of his life. Winter would come, but he would wait for spring, keen to continue living. But once he felt he was no longer needed, the hope and desire to live vanished – and the end was not far away.

It's a shame, but a lot of people think like this man. Their strength, health, beauty, and eyesight have been lost; their body no longer responds to their wishes; they are no longer themselves. And so, they give up.

But should we give up? Should we just stop and go away? If so, what was the meaning of coming into this world in the first place?

In Britain, the elderly rarely feel useless, and no one ever thinks of them as such. As an outsider arriving in Britain,

I found it remarkable that senior citizens were out in their cars and shuffling into the store with their walking frames. In Lithuania, by contrast, I have never seen the senior citizens, especially the elderly women, being so independent. In the UK, it is common and of no surprise to anyone. I really like this form of respect.

This approach helps to maintain a sense of purpose and usefulness in life, which can in turn help to prolong life.

The 19th century American philosopher, poet and essayist Ralph Waldo Emerson addressed this point when he wrote: "We do not count a man's years until he has nothing else to count."

I'll always remember one old lady whose optimism I admired. She enjoyed life and was very active. Insofar as she was able, she participated in the life of the Church and was engaged in charity work. When her fingers were able to move, she knitted blankets that the Church donated to deprived people. I can imagine how much love and good wishes that old woman put into the covers that she made. There seems to be something miraculous about such an attitude. I admired her and I admire people like her.

There is no such thing as a definite point beyond which death is inevitable. Any such limits can be shifted, depending on how we live our lives. The more active and meaningful a person's life is, the further the limits move forward, becoming blurred, until they disappear.

There are many elderly women who knit gloves, scarves and blankets for charity. Those items are so beautiful!

These women believe in their strength; they ask the nurses to bring pain-relief medicines – and then they continue to work. They are filled with ideas on how to help others and a willingness to put them into action. That type of old age is really a blessed old age.

Actually, far from being depressing, old age can be a time of inspiration for some lucky people. Towards the end of their life, some people are able to reflect on the wisdom they've accumulated and to share this with their children and grandchildren.

This is an idea emphasised by Joseph Murphy, the American cleric, preacher and philosopher, who said: "Age is not the flight of years; it is the dawn of wisdom in the mind of man."

Old age is not necessarily a tragedy. It is just an inevitable part of life, and it has always been that way. Old age is just a physical change in the body; a new step forward in our lives. It does not diminish what a person has had during the course of their life: beauty, wisdom, talent, strength, compassion, and many other wonderful attributes. There are many forces in the human mind that are stronger than the merely physical.

Raising the spirits

One of the more satisfying tasks of a nurse in a nursing home is helping with leisure activities aimed at lifting the spirits of the residents. This includes activities that residents would have enjoyed in their younger days: everything from singing and dancing, through to drawing pictures and playing games. This provides them with some enjoyable ways of passing the time, as well as reminding them of the happy times from their past.

Sometimes singers will visit a nursing home. They sing old songs, and the patients remember them, often singing along together. Dancers also visit, encouraging residents to join them in dancing to tunes that they knew in their youth. The aim is the same: to raise the spirits of the old and unwell.

Sometimes there is a visit by a mini-zoo, allowing residents a chance to stroke friendly animals, such as dogs, rabbits and guinea pigs. At the home where I work there is a soft, fluffy rabbit. He is loved by all the residents, and especially by those who are unable to leave their beds.

There are also visits by Church representatives, who help to nurture the residents' religious faith. This is particularly useful for those who find it difficult to leave the nursing home for visits to church.

Most people like bingo. A special machine is used to randomly select the numbers, and the residents mark these off their bingo cards. If one of them is lucky enough to get all the right numbers, they win the prize. It is a simple game, but it gives the residents a lot of fun and puts them in a good mood.

During festive occasions, charity raffles are held, with the prizes often donated by nursing home employees and the relatives and friends of patients. Staff and patients buy tickets for a nominal price, often just one pound. Everyone who has bought a ticket will wait with eager interest, keen to see who breaks out in a smile, a sure sign of success.

Sunday is movie day. Residents get to watch old films that they've loved. The stories, the actors and the music all take them back to happier times.

In combination, these various activities remind residents of the joy and fulfilment they experienced in the past, showing them that the same feelings can be rekindled in the present. It's a valuable lesson, and it can work wonders to blow away the blues.

At the nursing home where I currently work, some of the residents are very talented. For example, we have a talented artist. His paintings are hanging on the walls of his room. Since he had a stroke, he can no longer draw, but he still uses his pencil to colour children's books. I like to sit with him and watch him working, colouring the pictures.

He tells the stories of the origins of his paintings, what he painted and where. He talks about his sources of inspiration for each piece, including the people that he knew at the time. We both enjoy these discussions.

Although they may not be so talented, most residents at the home take part in drawing lessons at some point. During one such session, one woman drew two smiley faces inside a heart, and with a bright-eyed expression, she said to me: "This is you and me."

I was very excited and thanked her. In the evening, when I came to wish her a good night, I found her holding that picture and kissing it.

Another woman stricken with Parkinson's was happy to have created a postcard. I complimented her and she became even happier. She wrote some wonderful words on the postcard: "All you need is love." These were sensitive words, and very true.

It's great to see people forget about their age, focusing instead on gathering together all the good things of their life, getting every last drop of joy out of life – right down to the last drop in the well. In this respect, nurses often act as guardian angels for their patients, helping them live life to the full.

The power of love

Even at the sunset of life, even in nursing homes, people find each other, fall in love and become couples. One couple in particular stands out in my memory. An elderly woman had lost her speech after a stroke, while her male friend was over 90 years old. They really loved each other and wanted to get married. Their dream was interrupted by the man's death, but I believe that he left life happy, because until the last minute he felt responsible for the woman that Destiny had brought his way.

I remember another married couple who showed the power of love. The woman was disabled and the husband would come and visit her in the nursing home. Their faces would shine brightly with love when they met – a sort of radiance that I'd never seen before. It's hard to believe that a man could love a woman like that.

Having lived together for more than 60 years, this couple had often talked happily about their children, where they had worked and what they had achieved throughout their lives. And now, even though the wife could no longer speak, they still had the ability to communicate. I really believe that the language they spoke to one another was the language of mutual love and understanding.

Another lasting relationship illustrated the value of love as a source of strength. One morning I was bringing medicines to the residents as they sat in their armchairs, when I found myself in a funny situation. A man came to visit one of the women sitting there. He shouted out: "Well, how is the most beautiful girl in the world?"

His voice was full of joy, and I thought for a moment that the compliment was meant for me. But the man walked past me, went directly to his wife and kissed her. These words – the nicest, warmest of words – were for the love of his life.

"How beautiful!" I thought.

Those loving words made life worth living for them both. I knew that throughout the whole year, that deep feeling of mutual love allowed them to keep enjoying life.

Life and death

Working in a nursing home, I often get to know residents very well – learning many details about their long and interesting lives – only to find that I have to say a final farewell at the end.

My job involves lots of talking and listening, and many patients have told me the stories of their lives and loved ones. Very often, their children had emigrated to places like Canada, Australia, the USA and other countries. This has increased their opportunities for travel, but it has also put distance between themselves and those they love.

People have related to me the joyful and wonderful moments of their lives. Through their stories, I have travelled to many distant parts of the world. Many patients gave vivid accounts of their experiences and impressions. They also offered me advice on where to go, where to stay and what to see. I have travelled a lot with my husband, and I have much to tell my patients as well. We have often enjoyed sharing the experiences and impressions of our various travels and adventures.

I have been glad to hear stories of the loving relationships that have brought happiness to my patients, as well as the various accomplishments of which they're proud. It's good to share in other people's sense of satisfaction.

However, our exchanges have often had their sad side as well, and I have listened to many heart-breaking life experiences. Some of these patients were nearly a hundred years old, with no relatives to confide in, and so whatever sadness they felt was shared with the nursing staff. I often became tired of listening and felt a hidden grief for their loneliness. There were moments when I wanted to cry.

Once, I asked a very old lady, "Would you like some pain-killers?"

She answered, "Nurse, I'd rather you brought me a pill for death."

She didn't mean a pill to cure death, of course, but one to hurry it along.

Her name was Doris. She had a son Michael. There he received an attractive offer, but the contract conditions would require him to move to Australia. He agreed to go there, where he stayed for good. Now he, his work, his family and his house are all in Australia; but what about Doris? Years went by; Doris's husband passed away, and she was all alone. When it became too hard for her to do housework and arthritis began to limit almost all of her movements, she decided to move into a nursing home. Here she would be cared for and would have some companions at least. I became one of them, and Doris seemed to be especially fond of me. She would entrust me with her worries, ask for advice, and describe what she saw in her dreams. Her son couldn't fly from Australia to come and see his mother often. He was old too, so he would visit her once a year. She was happy even to have a conversation on the phone with him, though. Such conversations would make her day.

Nurses are generally reluctant to talk with patients about death. It is a painful and sensitive subject. The end of life is inevitable, but every patient has different ways of dealing with this fact. Some people are tired of living; they are sad, waiting for the end, immersed in apathy. Others take a more positive approach; they are able to be philosophical and enjoy life until the last moment – that final farewell.

Even so, it is never easy to say goodbye to those patients for whom I've cared, building a close relationship over time. Watching someone you care for slip away is difficult, although one can perhaps take comfort in the knowledge that they went out quietly, without pain, and without regrets.

In a way, death brings an additional burden for the care assistants and nursing staff. Due to our responsibilities, we must remain strong, even when we feel very sad. We may feel like crying at the death of someone we've cared for, but we know we must be strong for the sake of those around us. We must be strong and get on with the next task on the list.

At first, whenever I lost one of my patients or residents, I would get very upset. I would wonder about the meaning of life if it only ends in death. What was the point of all their hard work and struggling if it ends this way?

But over the years my attitude has changed. These days, I always think that the person who died has gone to a better world – and I pray for them.

Final thoughts

Looking back on my long journey from Latvia to life as a qualified nurse in England, I feel a great sense of accomplishment. Of course, many people have made similar journeys, but that does not lessen the importance of each individual journey.

My own story started with a dream, followed by another, and another. And finally, all of my dreams have come true. Now I am doing the job that I love in a country that has been good to me, providing work and a comfortable life for me and my husband.

This book is also the result of a dream: to share my experiences, not only as a migrant, but as someone who has witnessed a great deal of human suffering and done her best to alleviate it. I only hope that my readers will find something within these pages that interests and perhaps inspires them.

The training of a nurse is complex and difficult, and the daily routine can be exhausting. But no matter how competent you are in technical terms, this will never be enough if you fail to inject genuine caring into your work.

Particularly with the old and chronically ill, there is a need for tenderness, for extra care, for listening, and for making a difference. When the patient opens their eyes and sees a nurse or care assistant, their pain lessens. The patient always welcomes the nurse because the nurse makes the patient's life more meaningful.

Nursing staff must always try to be pleasant, and give kind and comforting words wherever possible. And yes, this relieves pain. So say most patients.

As a nurse, if you love your work, wherever the patient lives also becomes your own home. Likewise, the patients themselves become your family.

I am proud to work as a nurse in the UK. I am grateful to Fate and to God for the fact that everything came together. I am grateful that I found myself here, in this place.

Yes, it's Hard
When facing stress from nursing the sick and infirm, how can you withstand the pressure? I have been working as a caregiver in nursing homes in England since 2005. With the help of a recruitment agency, I have had the opportunity to work in over a hundred nursing homes, homes for the disabled, and caregiving centres.

My job is to care for unwell, terminally ill and dying patients, providing them with healthcare, socialising with them and doing everything possible to ensure they live out the rest of their life to the full, with a minimum of physical and emotional pain. Having spent years in this field, I have come to understand why people who nurse a sick family member, or a patient feel like their heart is crying. It's because it's hard. A caregiver helps those in pain, but who will soothe their pain?

I have lived through this pain, and I would like to talk about it by relating real-life examples. At the same time, you'll find an answer to the following question: How to avoid falling into depression when caring for the terminally ill?

The majority of my patients are close to a hundred years old. Their children live far away, and their children are old too, so they cannot visit their parents frequently.

The patients understand the situation, but they still feel lonely. They long for companionship and want to share their problems and dreams with somebody. So, we become their closest friends; we listen to their stories and talk with them about their lives and ours. Sometimes, we get tired from such stories, because each one of us has endured grief and loneliness, and at times I feel like crying together with the storyteller.

There was this ninety-eight-year-old lady called Maggie who used to live with her seventy-two-year-old daughter, Alice. The daughter was single; she didn't have a family and was working in an office. They had an ordinary life: work, home, and friends. When Maggie became sick, Alice left work and dedicated all her time to her mother. But something terrible happened: the daughter was diagnosed with cancer in her intestinal tract.

In England, people over fifty-five undergo a mandatory medical check-up every five years, which includes a colonoscopy. This is not the most pleasant procedure, but it's a necessary one, helping to detect polyps, ulcers and cancer. This is what happened with Alice. A tumour was found in her intestines during this procedure. She underwent treatment for two years, but to no avail. Alice passed away, and Maggie was placed in our nursing home.

We became her family. We knew how much pain she went through and admired her attitude towards life and people. She was an example for us in that she was hardworking and constantly needing to do something good. This amazing woman always wanted to be of help to somebody.

Maggie used to be an active member of a church community. From time to time, a pastor, nuns, and other members of their community would come to visit her. Each time they visited, she would give them knitted hats, gloves and toys for children. She knitted all that with her own hands, still finding ways to help others even from inside the nursing home.

There was this other patient, ninety-four-year-old Doris. When she was young, she'd had a colourful and active life. She was a rich businessman's wife; they loved equestrian sports and had their own horses. Her husband used to compete in races, and they had two wonderful sons.

Doris's life then was full of events: races, victories, prizes, cups, receptions and society. It seemed like a happy life that would last forever, but then the war broke out, and Doris lost her brothers and her eldest son. Doris never liked to talk about the war.

At that time, she started working in a hospital, caring for the wounded and trying to relieve their suffering. There she often saw death. In a sense, she was my colleague.

After the war Doris's younger son enrolled in a university, became an engineer and moved to Africa to work.

Of course, we cannot talk with our patients about death. Although the end is inevitable, this topic is too sensitive. However, each one reaches that finishing line in their own way. Some who are tired of life await the end with a sense of sadness, drowning in apathy; others rejoice in every second and have a philosophical view of life's farewell.

I won't conceal the truth: our work takes a heavy emotional toll. It's hard to part with people with whom you have grown close. Yes, that's hard. You can only comfort yourself and their relatives. You can only say they left this world quietly without pain and suffering, and that 'there' it will be better for them.

Is simply to be near them

It's not so important what exactly you are doing: reading, singing or whatever... The most important thing is simply to be near them. Soon, you will realise this closeness is comforting both to them and to you. Maybe it's even more of a comfort to you than to the patient. The ill person feels good just because they can hear a dear one's voice and see that one around them.

Often a nurse is actually the nearest and dearest person to a patient.

Patients and their relatives

A lot of stressful situations can be caused by the relatives of patients. Some of them just can't hear what you have to say, or they don't want to hear. They may shout or even threaten you. In situations like these, I just smile, keep calm and count to ten. I realise that in this moment the person is going through an inner struggle. Later, when they calm down, I explain the situation again and direct that person to the manager of our facilities.

Honestly, I do not always calm down quickly myself. Of course not! There have been occasions when I have gone to look for our manager ahead of the relatives, and in an outpouring of emotion would say that I'm leaving. In the end, though, I would always stay and continue working there.

Caring for the sick at home

When taking care of loved ones at home, we often make a huge mistake – we forget about ourselves. You should always remember:

YOUR LIFE HAS NOT ENDED

We are giving our best, giving all of ourselves to our loved one who, due to their illness, cannot even understand us and sometimes doesn't even recognise us. What happens when the one we care for leaves this world and we are all alone, though? Suddenly, out of nowhere, all kinds of illnesses and ailments befall us.

SOLDIERS GET SICK AFTER THE WAR.

I know of a woman who was nursing her sick mother for eight years. To spend more time with her, Maria left her job and dedicated her life to caring for her mother. When her mother died, she became very unwell herself. All of a sudden, the problems with her back and joints worsened. After that, Maria told her children not to make the same mistake: carrying the burden of nursing her mother alone and not accepting the help of others. She didn't want to burden others, and, finally, she became a terminally ill patient herself.

There is a saying: 'Soldiers don't get sick at war. Soldiers get sick after the war.' So, it is vital that you learn to accept the help of others in difficult times, or at least have someone to talk to and alleviate your burden.

WHETHER TO ACCEPT HELP OR NOT

All of us have pride. I have often noticed that the stronger a person looks outwardly, the more vulnerable they are deep inside. We cannot run away from our true self. This is when the classic question of 'To be or not to be?' arises. Remember, you can and you should seek help, and only you have the right to decide whether to accept this help or not.

When we don't want to accept any aid, it's our pride speaking. Sometimes, we should just push ourselves to accept help, to come to terms with the situation and admit our weakness. We have to do it for our own wellbeing, so we won't become a burden to our loved ones later.

An example from my life

My mother is eighty-two-years-old. I live far away from her in a different country. When she fell ill with cystitis, it started developing and the inflammation became quite dangerous. But she wouldn't go to the doctor: no way. At first, I could only advise her over the phone: what medication to take, what food to eat. I came after two weeks, as soon as I could. I was terrified when I saw her. She had lost six kilos, her face had turned grey, and she was disoriented. Even when talking with me, she couldn't understand what was going on around her. She would get confused, ask the same thing many times, and she wouldn't eat.

Of course, I immediately took her to the doctor, where she got good treatment, and, thank God, gradually recovered. What to do next, though? I realised that my mum needed someone to check on her and lend a hand around the house.

Socialising

Time spent socialising with others is really precious for those who nurse bedridden people and live for long periods in this gruelling routine. If you wonder how to support somebody who tends to the sick, just offer them a cup of tea and spend some time together. This alone will be of great help. When having a conversation, beware of giving general advice and explaining basic truths: your friend may feel as if you don't take their concerns seriously and push you away.

There are thoughts so deeply personal that you cannot express them, but after a chat, you feel relieved and comforted. At times, we may feel like there is no way out and nothing can help, least of all someone else's advice. I hope that by reading this book you will find a way to improve your life. If you know of a friend who has a bedridden person in their care, show them some empathy. It's hard work, both physically and emotionally. Having a bedridden person in your house is depressing; it's sad to see how your loved one is fading.

If you are the one caring for a sick or disabled person and cannot go out, don't hold back from inviting guests, friends and relatives to visit you. It will drive gloomy thoughts away and give both you and your loved one positive emotions. Some are afraid of making their relatives sad or of tiring the one who is unwell. Of course, people and situations differ. However, a visit from a guest makes the unwell ones pull themselves together. New faces guarantee a good mood and a feeling of normality. Praying can also be of great support. I have seen this many times and felt it personally.

Learn to find balance
It is easier for a person to face difficulties if they have other areas of interest which bring them joy. That is why it is so important not to let one single activity – such as nursing - take up all of your time. You need to have something to turn to, something that can give you energy and give meaning to your life: family, religion, a hobby or a

career. Here are a few pieces of advice which can help you reduce your burden and find balance in your life:

1. Admit that, despite all the irritation, inconveniences, problems and limitations you constantly face, taking care of this person was your personal, voluntary choice.

2. Concentrate on the positive aspects of your choice. Maybe by caring for your parents you are thanking them for their support and all they did for you when you were young. Perhaps you are doing it because this solution was the only possible, principled and appropriate choice given your circumstances. Or you may want to set a good example for your children. There are many reasons to be proud of yourself for this choice, and this can serve as a deep-rooted motivation for you to live through these difficult times and stay strong.

3. Don't worry about things which are out of your control. Concentrate on dealing with solvable problems. You cannot cure your mother's cancer, but you can ask your brother for assistance, so do it.

4. Look for moral support. Positive emotions and cheerfulness do not always come from the person you are nursing. If you feel that your efforts are underappreciated, reach out to friends and family who will listen and give you the credit you deserve.

5. Don't be shy of accepting help. Let others experience the joy of giving and feel good about supporting you. Create a list of small tasks which are easy to delegate,

such as getting the shopping or taking the unwell person to their doctor.

6. Sometimes, darkness and silence can help relieve emotional and psychological fatigue. Lie down, turn off the lights, cover yourself with a blanket and rest for a while.

7. Some people ease fatigue with the help of water. Take a shower, go to a swimming pool, or just lie in the bath. You could also enrol in an aqua-aerobics program. It's very good for your health, invigorating, and improves your physical and emotional wellbeing.

8. Personally, writing is the most helpful thing for me. I love describing my emotions, thoughts and reasoning, and making conclusions. I entrust my worries to paper and write about everything I cannot say out loud.

Ten points on how to stay positive
A correct and balanced view of yourself is all you need right now. There is no point in looking back. Don't be anxious about things you can't control. Don't let excessive worries build up in your mind. Try to be positive about your situation. Really, the most precious trait of successful people I've met is a positive outlook. Your attitude towards each specific situation determines how you will live. Learn to withstand negative feelings and turn negative points into positives. You don't want to destroy your nervous system, do you? Then do things that will help you stay calm and healthy.

1. Exercise or take up a sport. Visit a gym at least twice a week or have a jog. Have a regular exercise regime in the morning, or at least walk to work.

2. Have a healthy diet. Eat less fast food and other junk food. Eat more vegetables, fruits (especially bananas as they help increase the hormone of joy), and nuts.

3. Always get enough sleep. You should never sleep less than eight hours a day, as this is the amount of time our bodies need to restore their powers. Don't turn into a zombie constantly lacking sleep.

4. Have a schedule. Try to go to bed and get up at roughly the same time every day. Do the important and difficult tasks in the first half of the day when your mind is clear, and you have more energy.

5. Finish all work on time. Remember that one of the key reasons for stress is a pile of pending tasks.
6. Feed your brain not only with beneficial but also with pleasant information; alternate reading of fiction and non-fiction books.

7. Find your hobby. When you have an activity which interests you, you can always switch to it to escape from stress.

8. Spend plenty of time surrounded by nature. A touch of nature restores our strength.

9. Listen to music. A melody which is pleasant to your ears will brush away negative thoughts and help you relax.

10.   Surround yourself with pleasant aromas. Aroma-therapy is a powerful tool for fighting stress.

Patients often call us angels
There was one old lady who had dementia. She couldn't let go of the habit she'd had since her youth of using hair rollers, and she used to curl her hair with them every day. She didn't allow anyone to touch her hair. She knew and could recognise me, though, and she would let me help her with her rollers. It seems that she trusted me.

On another occasion, a patient suffering from dementia approached me and started crying. She said she couldn't remember anything. She felt like she should go some-where, but she couldn't recall where and with whom. She was so sincere in her tragedy I couldn't help crying with her. I tried to support her, or at least calm her down. I said that I was here and tried to help her recall where she was and what she was about to do. She kissed me on my cheek and said I was her angel.

Learn to listen

Each person has a secret in his or her life, especially if they have lived a long time. If their life ends unexpectedly, they bury their secrets with them. However, if they have lived till an advanced age and don't have the strength to bear it any longer, they try to leave their secrets here on Earth. Why? I don't really know. Maybe they think this way it will be easier to fly up.

Margaret's secret

Margaret knows that she has cancer and will die soon. She has a secret, though, and she doesn't want to take it with her. She doesn't have any children, so she decided to share this secret with me, her nurse.

When she was a child, Margaret was raped by a man who lived in her neighbourhood. After the incident, he moved away, but she was left with a psychological trauma that lasted for years. She was afraid of men and didn't have any interest in boys whatsoever. She finished school, graduated from university, began working, and became a leader of a scout youth group, organising different events. Margaret lost her job, but she didn't give up and started her own business. She began travelling abroad. During one of her trips, she spotted that very man who had raped her all those years ago. Could she be sure it was him, though? How many years had passed? "Maybe he just looks like him," she thought.

They were both scouts then and liked each other instantly. They began dating, and later they got married. However, as she got to know her husband better, she realised that he was definitely the man who had raped her. She wouldn't admit it to herself, though, because she had feelings for him. She was in love, and she couldn't admit the truth. They lived a long and wonderful life together. Margaret had everything: charm, talent, work she enjoyed, a social life, a rich and handsome husband... But she had a secret she concealed from everyone. Now, in old age, tired from her long illness, Margaret couldn't keep it any longer and decided to reveal it to me.

The release
Sitting in her armchair, Margaret was deep in thought. Her family had visited, bringing up memories of the past. I came as usual on my morning round, gave her pills and asked her how she was.

– 'Today is not the best day of the year,' she answered. 'It's the anniversary of my husband's death. I don't want to think about it, but my friends and family always remind me of this. They come and talk to me about Andrew, and I'm tired of such conversations.'

Margaret looks downhearted, but she wants to talk to me; she has decided to whom she will confess her secret. She asks me to sit down and begins her story by saying that her life was very rich. Whilst talking about it, she cheers up a bit, her memories carrying her into a past that was full of positive energy.

– 'I want to tell you the story of my life,' says Margaret. 'As each day goes and a new one comes, I feel I'm gradually falling into an abyss. I don't remember anything. I don't

170

understand what I'm doing at times. When the nurses tell me what I've done, I'm often surprised as I don't remember doing these things.'

Margaret looks at me confused, as if I am able to help her with something.

- 'I have a secret,' she told me, 'and I want to share this secret with you while I'm still able to recall it. I think that after I reveal it, I will feel much better.'

I said that I would listen to her secret a bit later when I have time as I'm in the middle of my rounds, but she said:

- 'No, listen now! I may not have time later.'

I promised to come back in five minutes and continue our conversation, but some guests came to see her, so our talk was delayed. We didn't manage to talk again that day, and after I finished work and went home, I kept thinking about Margaret, wondering what her story was.

The next morning when I came to work, the first thing I did was go to her. She was lying in bed and probably having a nap. I took her hand in mine. She squeezed my hand and said:

- 'I can feel your hand, but my hand is not a part of my body anymore; it's growing weaker.'

I reassured her and went to get some medicine. I helped Margaret wash her face, dressed her, and she had her breakfast. I had a few more patients waiting for me, so I told her I'd be back in thirty minutes and went to serve the other patients. When I finished, I ran back to Margaret. She looked better and was ready to tell me her story.

- 'I was born in Yorkshire into the family of a vicar,' she said. 'We were four siblings, and I was the eldest. Our family was not rich, and our parents worked hard to give us an education. I loved going to school. I enjoyed studying and playing with friends. One day, however, it all changed.'

Margaret closed her eyes and turned pale.

- 'Margaret, are you sure you want to continue talking about it?' I asked.

She opened her eyes, looked at me and smiled.

- 'One day as I was going home from school, a young man, about seventeen or eighteen years old approached me,' she continued. 'he said his dog had just given birth and he would show me the puppies. I loved dogs and wanted to have a puppy. I followed him, even though I didn't know exactly where he lived. We walked out of our town and headed to the forest. I became wary, but he gave me some logical reason why his dog was in the forest, so I believed him and we carried on walking. When we entered the forest, he assaulted me; started pressing himself on me. I was shouting and wriggling, but couldn't escape his strong hands. He raped me. I was nine years old.'

- 'When he was done, he left me in the forest. I was shaking and crying; I didn't know what to do. What would I say to my parents? I came home dirty, in tears, pitiful and, of course, I told them what had happened. My dad immediately went to the police. They started searching for this young man, and our neighbours and relatives tried to help. Alas, even with a description, nobody found him. I remembered one specific detail: just above his groin there was a tattoo with a year and the name – Andrew.'

- 'After this, my dreams were never the same as before. They were more and more realistic. I was always looking for something, and somebody was always spying on me. And men no longer existed for me.'

- 'Years passed. I opened a business. I had money and went on a cruise with a friend. During this journey I met many people, but my eyes kept fixating on one man. Something clicked inside me. Something was attracting me to him. I couldn't understand what was going on in my head. It could be that God had his own plan, and that man reciprocated my interest.'

- 'After the cruise, we started dating. My hatred towards men disappeared. I was deeply in love. Andrew, my boyfriend, was in love with me too. He was ten years older than me.'

- 'We got married, and it seemed this happiness would never end, until one day I saw a tattoo above his groin, a year and the name – Andrew. You know, in those days it wasn't acceptable for people to have relations before marriage, so on my wedding night I was just sinking in love and didn't examine his body. After some time, though, I saw the tattoo and was deeply shocked. Life seemed to have stopped, and memories of the past flooded my mind.'

- 'I couldn't believe myself. I was in love with him! With all my heart and mind, I told myself it was just a coincidence. I couldn't face it. As the years went by, though, logic prevailed.'

- 'One time, we were drinking tea and chatting about our past, and I realised the person in front of me was the guy who had assaulted me when I was nine. There was a searing pain in my heart, but I didn't feel any grudge, neither hate nor disdain. I was looking at him and thinking that we'd had a beautiful life together; we had true love and unity. We didn't have children, but it didn't affect our feelings for one another.'

– 'Then, Andrew passed away. I never told him about our early encounter. It was my secret. Now I'm leaving this world and I want to leave my secret here on Earth.'

After this conversation, Margaret lived for just a few more weeks. Maybe she felt better after revealing her secret to me. She died quietly and peacefully. She knew that she would meet with Andrew.

The painter

I love art, paintings and engravings very much. When I travel to different places, I always visit the local galleries and museums. Art has something so vast and limitless; it depicts moods in a unique way. Painting requires a great deal of attention, concentration, insight, curiosity and love, just as good music, a good book or good care do. Sometimes artists come to live in our nursing home due to their illnesses. One day, we welcomed a new patient whose name was George. Upon his request, his relatives came and filled the walls of his room with his paintings. In addition to these, he had a few albums with photos of his paintings, which he loved showing to us. Following a stroke, the right side of George's body was left paralysed. He tried to continue painting and found pleasure in talking about his paintings, though. One could see that these memories were carrying him far away. He looked so happy when talking about them that I became interested in his paintings and decided to take a closer look at them. George was excited to see my interest, and described his paintings to me in more detail: when, where and in what circumstances they were done. Each time I visited him during my breaks, I would bring him some English tea and have the pleasure of listening to his stories. George was always talking about his art.

There were a large number of paintings and my time was quite limited, so we would choose a theme; for example, the paintings of his house or marines. When George was describing how he was painting and how he felt during this process, his eyes would shine brightly. He said that art gave him strength, and George was a really strong man, like an old but solid tree.

In the course of my work, I become friends with my patients and quite often I'm with them until their last breath. When they pass away, I am left with good memories of them and can only wonder about this mysterious game called life. George was no exception. This game doesn't have any exceptions. He left this world, but he also left behind a part of himself in his paintings.

I have many friends who are painters. I particularly liked a comment by the painter, Ravil Abdulov, about my first book: 'I enjoyed reading your book, Aldona. It made me reflect on my life and think about whether I bring happiness, joy and something useful to other people's lives. I am a professional painter, and after reading your book I found an answer to my question. My thoughts and emotions are hidden inside of me; however, they come to light through colours and shapes.'

Conclusion

Dear readers! You are holding a wonderful book in your hands – a book which delves into questions about nursing the elderly. It's not easy to help your loved one and not neglect yourself at the same time. What moved me to write this book is the desire to help people see their situation in a new light and find a way out of difficult circumstances. Of course, personal development is the basis for everything; I have always been interested in how the mind works. I believe in human genius and think we are able to do much more than we think we can.

Table of contents